MW01681329

And I suppose we have to be thankful for Martin not fighting us anymore. At least now he is easier to handle. I can wash him and change his clothes without having help getting them off and back on again."

"But a lot of washing now, Ma," Annie told her softly, squeezing Addy's hand.

"Yes, from a man to a child, from a husband and a friend to a baby," Addy answered, wiping the sudden tears from her cheeks.

"And you're only forty-three years old," Linc commented

She shrugged, "What can I do about it? He would have taken care of me." And they all agreed.

Lost Love

Shirley Dummer

LOST LOVE

First Printing, 1994

International Standard Book Number 0-9633479-2-6

Printed in the United States of America

Dedicated to
my family, for their support,
encouragement and love.
And to my grandchildren
who think Grandma is awesome

Chapter I

"Addy, where's Pa going?"

"Ask him, not me! How should I know? He don't tell me anything anymore. I don't know anything anymore." Watching the man walking across the pasture toward the river, she wiped the tears starting to trickle down her cheeks with the inside of her fingers.

"Pa never walked before. Not if he could help it. He always rode Baldy. It seemed like his feet were never meant to touch the ground. And now he walks and walks. Funny!"

"Not so funny! And now he never changes clothes when he was always so fussy...so clean...really picky about being clean. Everyone else took a bath once a week in the winter, except Martin that is. He took a wash up so often that I felt like I was washing all the time too. And sometimes, it really made me mad when his clothes would end in the washbasket and they didn't look very dirty. Made me lots of extra wash. I'd give anything for those days again."

As they talked, they watched the man slowly disappear behind a hill in the far distance.

"Linc, I'm scared," Addy confessed. Linc shook his head

slowly, in total agreement. He realized that something was happening to his pa. Something was very wrong. He looked back at Addy still gazing into the distance. The ready laughter that had always come so easily was being replaced by lines of worry and uncertainty.

"What's going on? What you two looking at?" asked a second man coming to join them.

"Pa or the hill where Pa went. We just watched him walk across the pasture. He's gone behind that hill, now out of sight," Linc answered.

"Where you mean?"

"There," Linc answered, pointing into the distance. "There, toward the east. Behind that flock of sheep you see over there."

"Pa never liked walking before. He always rode Baldy."

"Ted, admit it. Get your head out of the clouds. We know you're in a dream world these days, but admit it anyway. Pa is changing. And it's not for the better, only worse," was Linc's sharp answer.

"And now he's got a temper, never know when it will fire off. He was always so even tempered before. Nothing stirred him up like it does now. He never flew off the handle, never hollered for nothing. Ted, you got to know something is wrong. You were there this morning when I wanted to wash his clothes. I laid the clean ones on his chair and took his dirty ones. He put the clean ones on all right, only came out into the kitchen before I could wash them and put the dirty ones on over the clean ones. And got real mad when I wanted him to take them back off. I thought for a minute he was going to hit me. You heard him," Addy said, her face a mixture of indignation yet with a hint of tears beginning again.

Ted finally shook his head yes in agreement. "I guess I have to agree, with what I saw and heard this morning. I guess I'm happy about getting married to Ruth and I don't want to put a cloud over that. Don't see much else or think about much else these days. Say, isn't that Ken and Pete I see going into the barn?"

"Oh yes," Addy sighed. "You were gone when they came home yesterday and when you came home last night they were already in bed and being gone today you don't know about the fighting in school yesterday. I didn't make them go to school today. Last day anyway so they don't miss much. One of the Kleeten boys, Joe, I guess, started to holler around about Martin. Heard it from home I suppose, said he was a crazy man, that they had a crazy man for a pa. Then one of the other boys, don't know which one, said their pa was in his second childhood, only he sure was mighty young for that. Of course, Ken hit him and then the whole pack of the boys started to hit Ken and Pete. Lucky for them, Mr. Landers saw it out of the window and went outside and broke it up. He don't put up with fighting much. Sent Ken and Pete home. And the rest, all of them, girls included cause they were egging it on by yelling about their pa being crazy, anyway they all had to go inside and sit at their desks. Ken had a bloody nose and bruises, besides torn pants and his shirt I threw away. Pete had bruises all over, a big one on his thigh and a black eye."

"Those Kleeten boys always liked to fight. Remember that from when I was in school. Older ones then. Lots of them, big family," Ted added.

"Addy, I hate to add this to the problems, but Ken and Pete sure have turned into liars. Or at least it seems that way," Linc told her.

"What you mean?"

"Well, I don't care how much they use the tools in Pa's shop, but everyone has to put them back. That was Pa's rule. And we always did just that cause Pa was strict about that. We're missing a hammer and a pliers, the best ones we had."

"You think the boys took them?" Addy asked.

"Had to," Linc replied, with Ted nodding his head.

"They are gone, Addy, and the boys say they did not take them. Who else would have? There ain't nobody else that goes in there," Linc said.

Sighing, Addy said, "I'll talk to them about it. They never

lied before. I'll talk to them , and I better get my wash folded too...and supper started."

"This has aged Addy a lot." Linc told his brother as they watched the woman walk away.

"It sure has. She was so good looking. Those big brown eyes and brown curly hair. And always a smile or a laugh. She don't look so happy nowadays. Some people hate their step-mothers, but I was always glad Pa married her. She made coming into the house a pleasure at meal time."

"How long they been married now?" Linc asked.

Ted shrugged his shoulders. "Maybe twelve, thirteen years. Yeah, must be thirteen years cause Ken is eleven and Pete nine now. With Annie going to have a baby, Pete won't be the baby anymore. How is Annie feeling, by the way?"

"Some better. I will be glad when the baby is born. Seems like she's been sick for so long," Linc replied.

"You remember Ruth's ma's sister, Rebecca?" Linc nodded his head yes, while Ted continued, "I kind of got the idea they had her lined up for you. They have said more than once how funny it was that you married your step-sister. Like you kind of got pushed into it by Addy and Pa."

"Hardly. Rebecca is the reason I quit going to the dances at Casson. I know you're going to marry into that family. Ever get the idea that they think they are better than we are?" Linc asked.

"What you mean?" Ted slowly asked.

"Don't get mad, but I always felt like they thought they were better than we were, better than lots of folks. I know they got a lot more money than most people do now with the depression, but that don't make them any better than anyone else," Linc answered.

"That's her pa, mostly," Ted replied. Then he slowly continued, "Well her ma sometimes too. Linc, we can't all marry an Annie. I told them that you never really looked at anyone else except Annie, but you had to wait until she grew up before Pa and Addy would let her even think about marrying. They didn't say anything more after that. Linc,

I'm twenty-five years old and want to settle down. I think Ruth and I will have a good home together."

"You got to live with her. As long as you're happy, guess that is what counts. Looks like Pa ain't coming back either. Let's get the chores done so we can eat supper on time. Think we'll have two cows to milk before long. Molly looks like she'll have her calf real soon."

Long after supper was eaten, dishes done and the rest of the family settled in their beds, Addy was still waiting for Martin to return. Knowing sleep wasn't going to come before he came back, she took a jacket from the hook by the door and went outside, settling herself comfortably on the steps with her tired back resting against the porch railing. The cattle dog, Shep, a very affectionate collie, settled by her feet. The day's work finally catching up with Addy, her eyes slowly closed and she drifted into uneasy dozing. Sometime later, she was startled when she felt a hand on her shoulder and heard Shep's gentle swishing of the tail.

"Martin?" she questioned.

"Who else? Why ain't you in bed?"

"Cause I worried about you. You ain't had no supper and it's late." Rising, she went into the house. "I'll go fix you something now. Won't take long to stoke the fire and heat some potatoes and fry some bacon."

"Don't bother," was the blunt reply.

"No bother. It won't take long." She felt his hand roughly closing on her arm.

"Go to bed," Martin shouted.

"All right," she whispered as he let go her arm. Fighting tears, she went into the bedroom. She could see to undress as the rays from the kitchen lamp shown through the open bedroom door. Listening to the cupboard doors being slammed, she settled in bed, finally going to sleep.

When the first signs of morning peeped through the bedroom window, Addy awoke and rolled over to the other side of the bed to find Martin asleep on the rug. Still in the same clothes he had worn the day before, his gentle snoring carried through the room.

Knowing she didn't have enough bread for breakfast, Addy quickly dressed and went into the kitchen. After carrying out the ashes from the stove, she stoked up the fire and put on a pan of milk to scald for the bread she had to bake. Taking out the ingredients needed, she made a large pan of baking powder biscuits. While the biscuits were baking, she made the dough for the bread. By this time, Ted had roused Ken and Pete so they could do their chores.

Addy had barely gotten the bread kneaded and the milk gravy made for the biscuits before they were back into the house sitting around the table ready to eat.

"You got those lambs bottle fed, Pete?" Ted asked.

"Yep, and they all ate real good. That one with so much black is funny. He'll bunt me all over if I don't watch it."

"Chickens fed, Ken?" the boy was asked.

"I threw some wheat out and I put water in the waterers for them," was the answer.

"Good. Biscuits are good, Addy," Ted complimented her.

"Thank you," Addy replied, a smile lighting up her face.

"Pa up yet?" Ted asked.

"No," She answered shaking her head.

"What time he come back last night?"

"Late. It looked like he ate dry bread for his supper. I made butter after our supper last night and that wasn't sliced into. And the jelly jar hadn't been opened either." She caught a quick look from Ted and added, "I offered to make him potatoes and fry some bacon, but he told me to go to bed."

"I heard him," Ken piped up. "He hollered at you to go to bed."

"And that is what I did," Addy said.

"Yeah," was Ted's answer as he shrugged his shoulders. Then he asked Ken and Pete, "More biscuits, boys? Got a lot of work to do today." And as Ted outlined what he thought should be done, Addy's thoughts were of the good looking family she had. There was no mistaking Ted and

Pete for brothers. They had the same light blonde hair, deep blue eyes and round face of their pa's. The facial expressions and gestures were so like Martin's. Ken and Annie look like me, she thought, my brown eyes and the same brown curly hair. Only Linc was different. The first time she had seen him, she had wondered who he had taken after and Martin had answered, "His ma." His black hair, longer face and greenish eyes set him apart from the rest.

Although they did not look alike both Linc and Ted had their pa's same thinking. Even the younger boys showed some of the same characteristics of Martin's. The precise clear headed, even tempered thinking had made him a top-notch rancher. Never one to make many mistakes, Martin's thoughts could be as sharp as a whiplash, honest, yet like steel once his mind was made up.

He had taken a very small ranch and had carved it into a nice size holding that they all were very proud of. The smaller acreage on this side of Blaze River was so suitable for the raising of winter wheat and hay while the prairie land on the other side of the river had been best suited for cattle grazing.

When Linc had been twenty-four, they had had the opportunity to buy another ranch that adjoined the one Martin owned. The young rancher had been digging a dam, hoping to guarantee water for his cattle. Owning one of the first tractors in the area, he had used it to do some of the digging. Getting too near the edge of the soft dirt, one side had mired down, making the tractor tip over pinning the man under one of the metal wheels. Finding him, his young wife had walked across the prairie calling for help. Martin and Linc had heard her screaming cries. Going back with her they got the tractor upright and off the body. After the undertaker had come, they had assisted him in loading the body in the hearse.

"You got a tractor like that?" he asked Martin.

"We ain't got any tractors yet. I've thought about getting one. They would be a help in working up the ground in the spring and again in late summer when we're putting in winter wheat."

"What kind is this?" he was asked.

"A 1930 Allis-Chalmers U. He just got it about two months ago. Wanted it to work on this here dam mostly and for working up winter wheat ground."

"Nice looking tractor," the undertaker commented.

"Yes, it is. Those metal lugs on those wheels dig in when you need traction. But that is what killed him too."

"Yeah. That would put holes in anyone's body when they go over it," the undertaker agreed, getting into the hearse.

The morning of the funeral, the young widow and her pa came to see Rafferty's. She asked Martin to buy the ranch just as it stood. This would include the cattle, machinery and everything in the buildings except furniture. Martin told her the decision would be made that evening and she would be told of their decision the following day.

"But Pa," Linc had argued, when Martin had told him that this would be his ranch. "The money you're going to buy this with is part of Addy's inheritance from her grandpa."

"Part of it," Addy agreed.

"I'll bet it's damn near all of it."

"No, only part of it."

"To make you feel better, we're going to take care of that," Martin told him. "We'll put the ranch in your and Addy's name. You'll do the work and Addy will put up the money." Addy shook her head in agreement.

"And Ted, when you get older, we'll do something for you too, but for now you're only twenty-two and sure ain't ready to settle down. The biggest thing in your head is what hell you can raise on a Saturday night. And," Martin continued, "I want something else done now while we're paying that lawyer, giving him money. I want Addy's name on the deed to this here ranch. Don't know why I waited this long to take care of it. My memory ain't dimmed to the struggles I had when Pa died. Paid that lawyer plenty to straighten out that mess. Had to pay off my two sisters and their being egged on by their husbands. Ain't gonna do that to my own kin. My sister said that when I died she would get this ranch back...take it back, and that ain't gonna happen. So I think I'll take my name off of here completely."

The first obstacle Martin had to overcome was the lawyer's objection to taking Martin's name off the deed and putting only Addy's on.

"You do remember how my sisters were?" Martin asked. Shaking his head yes, the lawyer finally agreed to Martin's selling the ranch to Addy for $1.00. But he did get a provision added that gave Martin a life estate, guaranteeing him the right to live there the rest of his life. After a great deal of thought, Martin also sold the cattle and machinery to Addy for the grand sum of $1.00. The provision was added to this sale making Addy responsible for Martin's well being for the rest of his days. Only when this had been added, was the lawyer satisfied that Martin's future was taken care of.

Addy had then made out a will, making the four sons the beneficiaries. Knowing Annie would inherit it when Addy's grandma on her mother's side died, Addy left her a small sum of money. And considering how Martin was now, Addy was glad this had all been done.

"Addy?" Ted waved his hand before her face. "I'm the one being told all the time that I've got my head in the clouds, but you sure haven't been with us for a while."

"Sorry, you want to tell me something?"

"Only where we'll be today, should you want us for anything. I'm taking Ken and we're gonna string wire on that fence we're making down by the river. Pete is gonna ride back to the other pasture with Shep and bring in that bunch of cows so they calf closer to the buildings."

"Sure hope we can help take them up to the High Ranch," Pete said.

"I imagine you will," Ted assured him. "Here comes Linc. He was going into Casson this morning early, to the mill to get salt. Wonder what he wants cause he sure never went."

"Glad I caught you all here," Linc said. "Got a cup of coffee left, Addy?" Getting it for him, she poured more for Ted and herself.

"Thought you were going into town this morning, nice, bright and early," Ted asked.

"Had a visitor this morning, nice, bright and early. Pa up this morning?"

Addy shook her head no.

"Damn. Joe Dakton was over this morning. He came down to the barn, thinking maybe Pa would be there. He wants to sell Pa half of his ranch. If Pa will buy this half, he has a buyer for the other half."

"I heard he was going to sell," Ted commented.

"How you know that? I first heard about it now," Linc said.

"Heard it from Ruth's pa the other night. He didn't tell me, but I heard him on the phone saying he thought it would be up for sale. I didn't mention it cause I thought he'd sell all of it in one chunk, instead of splitting it up."

"He wants to move away," Linc added.

"I wonder what Martin would say?" Addy asked.

"I don't know. He's so different than he was when you and I bought the High Ranch."

"This might be the time for Ted to get this land," Addy said, "I got money left and he and I could do the same with that land title as I did with you, Linc. I know Martin hasn't money enough to buy it alone."

"You doing the books now?" Linc asked.

"Yes. He hasn't been doing them for about six months now. I worked on them the other night when I couldn't sleep."

"You know this could solve where Ruth and I will live," Ted told them.

"Yes," Addy agreed. "There are buildings there. The house ain't too great, but in time it could be fixed up."

"Well, I kind of thought maybe you and Pa could live there and Ruth and I here cause then I'd be near the work."

"Damn it, Addy," Linc shouted, moving quickly out of

Addy's way as she dumped her coffee all over the table.

"Sorry...guess it just slipped out of my hand. I...say that again Ted...I don't think I heard right," Addy said.

"Addy," Linc started to say. Then seeing her staring at Ted, he got up and found a towel to wipe up the spilled coffee.

"Well, it was just a thought," Ted said. "You know we're the ones doing the work now or most of it cause Ken and Pete go to school mostly and Pa ain't doing nothing now but walking. Ruth and I could live here, and Pa and Addy could move up there, along with Ken and Pete."

"And Addy and Pa and Ken and Pete move up there?" Linc repeated glaring at his brother. "Addy took some of the money she inherited and painted and papered this house and put a roof on it and new siding. And paid for Pa to put in a new well and paid for Pa to put in a pump so she'd have water in the house. And now they should just move out and into that old house and let you have this one. What's the matter with you starting out in something like the rest of us? Annie and I live in a fixed up old shack. We hope in time to fix it up lots more, but for now it's nothing to brag about. Sure not like this house. What the hell makes you think you've got the right to take what Pa and Addy took years to get this nice? If its good enough for Annie and me to live down in our shack, then that old house up on the Big Mile Ranch would be plenty good enough for you and Ruth. What's good enough for me, little brother, is good enough for you."

"Sorry Addy, but Ruth is used to nice things."

"Then move to town and get a job so she can be supported in the style that she's used to," was Linc's razor sharp answer.

"There ain't no jobs there in town. You know this is 1930 and there just ain't no jobs to be had."

"You've looked?" Linc asked.

"Yeah," Ted slowly answered. "I've looked and there ain't any jobs to be had. At least for someone like me that ain't got no further than seventh grade."

"Then be happy with what you've got. And she had damn well better be too."

"Don't swear at my Ruth," Ted told Linc.

"Just don't expect Addy to pay for a ranch for youand then expect to boot her out of her home too. Come on Ken and Pete," Linc said as he slammed on his hat before closing the screen door with a bang.

"Ruth is different, Addy," Ted said looking sheepishly at his coffee cup. "Different from you and Annie. She comes from a nicer home. Not that this isn't nice, but they got fancier parlors and furniture and well, just everything. Like nicer curtains, real lacy and frilly."

"And two hired girls to wash and iron them too," Addy dryly told him.

"I know they have. I wish I could get a job in town that paid well, that would give me the money to give her what she is used to."

"But Ted, you are forgetting something. A woman should take what a man provides for her. Life on a ranch is not what it is in town. You are a rancher, a born one and a good one. Have always been and always wanted to be, until now. A woman should be willing to go where you go and make a home for you whether you live in town or out here. Otherwise, you had better take another look before you marry her. Or get a job somewhere else. Just don't go back and tell her I said that though," she cautioned.

"I won't. Addy, this getting married is supposed to be happy. Linc was happy when he was getting married."

"But he knew Annie would be happy with what he had to offer her."

"I been worrying for a time already about where we'll live. I know she'd be pleased with this house. Everyone thought I had my head in the clouds about getting married, but I've been worried about where we're going to live and about working somewhere else."

"I ain't gonna move from here, Ted. So get that straight through your head. You and Ruth had better know that now. I got enough on my mind with your pa now without thinking about something like that. I doubt if Martin would even think about it. Some days he's good and some days he ain't. Like yesterday, he was sharp tongued and I can't see talking to him about much of anything when he's like that. A couple of days ago he was better, but still not clear thinking like he used to be."

"What about the land?" Ted asked.

"Do you want your name on any land, Ted?"

"I don't know. Maybe we could paint and paper that house and make it look all right."

"Where you gonna get the money to do that?"

"I think her pa would give it to her if she asked him," Ted answered.

"I would feel better getting my money out of that bank. I know Jessie Anderson was here last week and she said after Dan sold all those cattle, he took the money home and they hid it. And that information is not to go anywhere else. I mean it. Don't tell anyone else. Except Linc. But not Ken or Pete or Ruth or anyone else." He shook his head no. "I think of how hard my grandpa and grandma worked," Addy continued, "and saved and I would really feel bad if that money got lost if that bank closed. Not only that, land would be a good place to put it. Martin always felt the land was a good place to put money."

"Pa wouldn't sign anything then," Ted asked.

"No and with my name on it, I would know my money would be safe, the ranch I mean."

"I wouldn't sell it out from under you," Ted assured her, getting up to go outside. Just the same, Addy thought as he went out the door, with my name on it, there wouldn't be a chance for you to sell it without my say-so. I just wish Ted had found somebody else to marry. She's going to be bad, I'm afraid. Sometimes I wonder if Ted is just getting married because he is tired of running around. My marriage to Frank was pushed by Pa and Ma. For my security, my good, they always said. What a letdown after the everyday living began, day after day. And I'm afraid Ted is going to find out what that kind of life is all about too.

Frank provided for me, but it was hard, once the newness of a home wore off. After he died, he left me with nothing. I was lucky I found that housekeeping job right away. Ted is going to find out Ruth is a different kettle of fish and her family even more difficult after the rope gets tied good and tight. And she's not even good-looking to make the bargain worse. Already she is pretty heavy and as she gets older and has her family, she sure will be as fat as her ma is now. I'd have sure picked a different daughter-in-law.

Within a week the transaction was completed. Coming down with the summer complaint and being bedridden, Ted asked Linc to make the arrangements with Joe Dakton on Big Mile Ranch. After an agreement had been reached on the price, a lawyer from Linksfort, Walter Talor, had taken care of the rest of the details involved in transferring ownership of the land. Before the final papers were signed, Addy and Linc had made the trip into Cassville and removed the balance of the inheritance from the bank. Taking only what was needed for the payment, she and Linc had carefully buried the rest in coffee cans in the dirt under some boards in the granary. Although she knew there would be no interest earned on this money, Addy still felt secure knowing it was not in some bank. The drifts of information on banks closing here and there made her happy knowing where her money was.

Through the week when this was going on, Addy had tried to talk to Martin about the buying of the ranch and had gotten no response. He plainly was not interested.

"I tried too, Addy," Ted told her several days after the papers were signed. "Kind of hurts when he was so interested in seeing Linc get his land."

"He wasn't sick then or whatever is the matter, Ted. If he was his old self, he would have been really pleased. I know he would have been."

"The funniest thing about all of this and it really ain't funny, is that Ruth's pa is not happy about my getting this ranch. He blew up about it when I told him we had signed the papers Friday. You know I went into Casson to see

Ruth last Friday night. Seems he wanted that land himself. And seems Dakton knew it too. But he didn't feel like selling the land to Mr. Patton. I also found out before he quit fuming that he didn't want us to buy, or you and Linc that is, to get High Ranch either. From what Ruth said afterwards her pa figured the widow would be up against it and have to take the first bidder for the ranch and her pa intended to buy it dirt cheap. Then when we got it, or you and Linc got it, he was real mad. I said that ain't very nice, cheating a widow out of money. And Ruth said I didn't understand money and banking cause that's how they make their money. What's the difference anyhow, she said, cause the widow was moving back with her people and they would take care of her."

"Your pa and I wondered about that before. Something was mentioned before on that, can't remember who said it, anyway we heard it and now that you mention it, it does bring back memories. I would have thought they wouldn't mind your owning Joe's Big Mile Ranch cause you're going to be in the family."

"Well, not really. If I owned it myself then Mr. Patton could have sold it for a profit. Ruth said her pa would find a buyer for it and make money on it."

"Even if you didn't want to sell it?" Addy asked.

Shrugging his shoulders, Ted answered, "When I told her you had a partnership in it, that was a different story. Cause then Mr. Patton couldn't sell it without your signature and how much could I influence you to sign it off?"

"And how about living up there, Ted? Have you mentioned anything to her about that?"

"No. Cause I can see that it just won't work. I met their other son-in-law last Friday night. He's a banker too, just like Ruth's pa. I have never felt so looked down on in my life. Ruth just laughed about it and said after her pa got done refining me, that I'd be just as good as they are."

"And," Addy asked with raised eyebrows, "how are they going to refine you?"

"I don't know. Oh Addy, what am I getting into?" Ted

asked.

"You had better know what you are getting into before you get into it. One good thing about all this is that you're finding all this out before instead of after. Ted, I'm going to tell you something I have never told anyone and that includes Martin. Don't marry just for the sake of getting married, just because you're tired of running around, going out on Saturday nights and because Linc is going to be a pa and has all the comforts of home. My pa and my ma pushed me into a marriage that was going to give me security, a home of my own and a secure life. It ain't that great," Addy told him, her head shaking no while she was talking. "After the newness of a home of my own faded away, all I found was myself living with a man I did not really care about. And it ain't very nice. I tried to make sure Frank never really knew how I felt. He had a housekeeper to keep his house clean, cook his meals, wash his clothes and in return I had a roof over my head. Now compared to what I have or had with Martin, there is no comparison. What I am saying is, be sure before you marry Ruth. It's a long life looking ahead if it ain't the right person."

"They think different than we do."

"Do they ever mention Martin or ask how he is?"

"Not in so many words," Ted answered. "But it's there, that feeling that my pa is not right in the head, going into second childhood. Little bits and pieces point to their thinking that. Got to get Ted out of there before some of it rubs off on him sort of thing."

"Like I said, Ted. Be careful and be sure."

"I have thought and thought until I can't think no more, Addy. Linc and I are going up, guess Ken and Pete too, anyway we're going up to Big Mile Ranch tomorrow and go through those buildings. See what is really in them and how much fixing they need. I'm going to take along a little food and stay there for a couple of days or longer. Maybe then it will hit me what to do."

"You are all going tomorrow?" Addy asked.

"Yeah, right after breakfast. Going to drive some cattle

up there to start summer pasturing. Linc, Ken and Pete are going to come back tomorrow night. I hadn't even thought about it before, but think it will do me good to go away by myself for a couple of days. Maybe I'll come back knowing what to do. And I hate to have to mention this, but some more tools were laying around the barn this morning. The boys said they put back what they used so it couldn't be them, but who else?"

"All right, I'll talk again to them, but when they say they don't do it, am I supposed to downright call them liars?" Addy asked as Ted shrugged his shoulders.

Ted stayed three weeks at Big Mile Ranch. During this time Addy noticed a distinct change in Martin. In the days when his health had been excellent his speech had been moderately even, his voice and his thinking precise. The past days his words were slurred and many times it seemed as if he were at a loss for wording.

Addy had no idea how to handle the terrible temper that seemed to be getting even more violent. Hearing a commotion on the porch one afternoon, she stood in dismay as she watched Martin take a favorite chair and deliberately smash it again and again against the porch railing. After the chair was demolished into bits and pieces he seemed satisfied and strode down the steps to begin his usual walk across the prairie and down along the river bottoms. Annie found Addy several minutes later sitting beside the broken chair, her head in her hands as she wept tears of frustration and discouragement.

"Ma, what happened?" she asked.

"Martin just broke that chair in pieces, his favorite one that he always sat in if he had time on Sundays and at the end of a day. He just smashed it against the railing, until, well, look at it now."

"His mind is going, Ma. Can't be nothing else."

"And how bad is it going to get? I wonder how we'll be able to live with it? What will we do with him?" Addy asked her daughter.

"Ma, you notice anything different about the people in

Casson when you go?"

"What you mean? I ain't been there for about a month now."

"Linc said when he went in to get a pair of shoes, cause his won't stay together anymore, the clerks in Peterson's Men's Store wouldn't wait on him. He finally left without getting the shoes."

"We gonna have that too?" Addy wondered.

"Maybe Linc was imagining it." Annie finally said, "I'm going down to the garden to pull some onion. You need any?" When Addy shook her head no, Annie left her to clean up the broken pieces of chair.

Something Dan Anderson said to Linc several days later gave Linc an inkling why Ted hadn't been able to find a job in Casson. Knowing there was an opening coming at the feed mill because of a sudden death of one of the employees, Dan had made the comment that probably he'd see Ted Raggerty's face there before very long.

"How come Ted didn't get the job then?" Linc asked.

"John looked kind of funny and said he had someone else in mind for the job. I said I had heard Ted was looking for a job and since Patton's bank had the loan on the feed mill, and everyone knew it, and since Ted was going to marry his daughter, I would have thought he would be the right one for the job. Sure couldn't see how he could not help but get the job. Patton told John he didn't want Ted hired there. He had something else in mind for Ted to do. He intended to get Ted into the bank and teach him the banking trade."

"Oh, that's news to me. I suppose that's how Ted is going to be refined. I wonder how Ted will like being cooped up all day in a bank, cause he always liked the ranch and being outdoors. Couldn't hardly keep him in school cause he wanted to spend all his time out of doors, especially in the spring," Linc answered.

"John said if he wanted to marry Ruth, then he'd have to do as Patton said or he wouldn't let her marry him. And John added, that's not for you to tell tales about to anyone.

Guess Patton thought with Ted's ranching experience he could be a help to Patton, providing he could fine tune the flaws and rough spots. Get him to be less clean thinking, make him realize that you have to take advantages at every lever you can."

"In other words, fleece widows out of their ranches," Linc commented.

Dan waited for Linc to clarify that statement and when he didn't Dan asked what he meant.

"Ted got an earful when Patton found out he and Addy bought part of Big Mile Ranch. He also found out he wasn't too pleased when we bought High Ranch either. Ruth told Ted that her pa figured to buy that one dirt cheap and make money reselling it. Didn't feel bad that the widow wouldn't get anything out of it cause she was going back to her people anyway. I think Ruth is as bad as her old man."

"And Ted is going to marry into that kind of a people?" Dan asked.

"He's thinking lots and lots. He's gone up to Big Mile Ranch now for a couple of weeks already. Guess its been that long. I think Addy talked to him plenty before he went. If Pa were only able, he'd give Ted some guidance too, but that's a lost cause. He only gets worse and worse. The feeling is there whenever I go into Casson that no one wants to talk to me anymore. I got it at the feed mill and at the Peterson's Men store."

"It's going round. It's a scare movement, that Martin is going crazy and you don't know what he'll do next and probably the rest of the family is going to do the same. And if you're smart you won't talk to them or let anyone see you talking to them," Dan told him.

"It is?" Linc asked, astonishment is his voice. "Why and who? Hell, old lady Patton was nuts before she died, our present banker's ma, and I know several that were childish before they died. Who is doing this to us?"

"I've been told it by several neighbors, Clintons and Darwins are some that are saying this. I've been warned by both of them. If I happen to hear any more I'll let you know.

You realize that the bank holds loans for their ranches."

"Yeah, I know. It's nice to know we've got one friend left anyway. Glad we don't have a loan at Patton's bank," Linc answered.

"Martin was damn good to me many times. And I worked with him too many times not to keep that friendship," Dan replied.

"Going to be hard for you talking to us?" Linc asked.

"Don't care if it is. There's plenty in Casson I don't care for. And our church is in Linksfort so we go there when we can. Wouldn't hurt me to thumb my nose at the whole Casson town. Just have to stock up more if I decide to spend my money in Linksfort. Most of my people and the missis' people are there anyway."

Addy figured her troubles were as large as she could handle, but she was to find out more were going to come her way very soon. School was to start the day after Labor Day. Exactly one week before, the school board visited her, Ray Patton, brother of the banker in Casson, Charles Boyen and Herman Clark. Boyen and Clark were brother-in-laws who owned and operated a ranch west of Rafferty's. Although very polite their request was firm and definite. Addy was not to send Ken and Pete to school the following week.

"We will not be responsible for any actions if your boys show up in school," Patton told Addy. "We know there was a fight right before school was out. Mr. Lander has other things to do, than to break up fighting in the school. We are afraid there will be a problem if you allow your boys to come."

"We would rather you did not, Mrs. Rafferty. I don't want bad feelings between neighbors with our ranch laying west of yours, but you know how boys are. We are afraid there will be trouble and we want to avoid this at all cost," Boyen added, "If we could talk to Martin, I am sure he would understand."

"He ain't here," Addy flatly told them.

"If you'll be good enough to pass the word along to him of our visit, I am sure he will understand," Herman Clark said. "We know your boys need their schooling."

"That's generous of you to understand that," Addy's brown eyes flashed.

"Well, we hoped you would understand that we are wanting to avoid trouble. As Herman was going to say, we would allow you to come and get the books needed for them this year and you could teach them yourself."

"I ain't no teacher," Addy told them.

"But we thought that you could probably teach them all they needed to learn. Just so they can keep up with the rest in their grade."

"I'll think about it," Addy told them. "And you gentlemen will excuse me if I don't offer you any coffee. I just don't feel like sharing anything with you right now. Coffee is meant to be shared with friends and neighbors and somehow I don't feel like you are anymore."

"Well, yes...I guess we'd better be on our way. You do understand, Mrs. Rafferty, this hasn't been easy for us."

"I feel so sorry for you," Addy told them as she held the door open for them to leave.

After they left, Addy sat on the porch steps staring into the distant hills. Somewhere near supper, Ted having ended his long stay at High Mile Ranch, rode into the yard.

"Another bad day, Addy?" he asked coming onto the porch after putting his horse in the corral.

"Yes, another bad day. Ted! Go down to Linc's and tell Annie and Linc to come up here. I don't care what they are doing. We are going to have a family talk. Ken and Pete, find them too. They might as well know what is going on cause this will affect them plenty."

"I was going into town tonight to see Ruth so hope this won't be too long," Ted told her going back down the path toward Linc's house.

"What's going on, Ma? I've got potatoes about done frying on the stove that I'm going to add some eggs to. Bread in the oven too," Annie added, "Ted thought you looked mad."

"Yes I'm mad, angry, insulted, disgusted and yes, very, very angry. I had company this afternoon, no, visitors, cause company is people you like and are friends. These were visitors. Three of the school board of our nice school here. Mr. Ray Patton, brother of your father-in-law to be was the ring leader," she told Ted. "The other two were Herman Clark and Charles Boyen. My two sons are not welcome at their school. Patton told me this while the other two nodded their heads in agreement. Don't want any fighting in school and my two sons will be causing the fighting. Not the rest of the bunch...only my two boys."

"How will they learn this fall, Ma?" Annie asked.

"Oh I am allowed to get their books so they can keep up with the rest of their class."

"You're no teacher," Ted said.

"That makes no difference."

"The School Board wants no fighting, no problems?" Linc asked.

"They will not be responsible for what will happen should the boys show up in school?" Ted asked.

"We didn't want to go back anyway," Kenny said. "Some of those boys, especially the Kleetens said some awful mean things about Pa last spring."

"And that's supposed to be all right," Addy said so angry she could hardly speak coherently.

"What names did they call you?" Ted asked the two boys.

"Names like crazy man's kid and loony birds," Pete answered.

"Sit down, Ted," Addy told him when he got up so suddenly the chair went flying. "Sit down, I've had a few hours to think about this before you came home."

"Just a minute, Ma. Don't you say another word cause I've got to take care of my potatoes and look at my bread."

"Bring them up here," Linc told her. I'll help you. With what Addy can find, we'll make our meal. Ted wants to go in to see Ruth tonight and I think that should be done so that is over with."

"Good," Addy told Ted, nodding her head in agreement. "I had made up my mind before I came home to this. And this would have definitely made it up for me. Ray Patton is a powerful man. Joe Patton runs the bank, but I think Ray is the one with the brains."

"Both got money though," Linc added.

Several minutes later the fried potatoes, eggs and fresh bread were joined on the table with what could be found in Addy's pantry, cobbling together a meal. Filling their plates, a few minutes was spent on satisfying the first stages of hunger.

"Now continue, Ma," Annie told her. "You ain't eating anything."

"Maybe later. Right now, I just can't. Before I felt helpless. Now I'm mad."

Looking at Annie she asked, "Do you remember those two brothers that used to work for your Pa?"

"Some. Their name was Packer, Parker..."

"Parker," Addy told her. Annie nodded her head in agreement, "I almost had it right."

"I got a letter from my Aunt Elsie when mail was gotten the other day and she said one of them had died, but the other one had lost his job at a ranch he was working at. The ranch had been sold. They went there the year your pa died. I want to hire him. They had a sister who was an old maid, a school teacher, and she had been replaced, kicked out by the school board for a man teacher. Guess they felt she could go live with her brother. The man teacher they hired needed the job worse than she did. And I guess they had some 15 and 16 year old boys in that school she had trouble with and the man they hired would make them mind. So she has no job. I want to hire her and if I can get which ever brother is still alive, I want to hire him too. I don't remember the woman's name, but will write to Aunt Elsie and get it. In fact, I will write the letter this evening yet and someone can make a trip to town and mail it tomorrow."

"I can see where you need a teacher, Addy, but why hire

her brother too?" Ted asked.

"If I can get the woman to come and teach, then maybe she would do some of the cooking and housework too. It would help me. It is getting harder and harder with Martin. He is gone everyday, God only knows where. I wonder sometimes if he don't come back for so long cause he gets lost. Shep used to go with him, but he won't go now and I wonder if Martin was mean to him, like he was to that chair."

"What chair, Addy?" Ted asked.

"Pa smashed his favorite chair all to bits one afternoon on the porch railing," Linc told him. "I told Ted what Dan Anderson told me that day too."

"Good. At least he knows what he almost married into," Addy answered, adding, "Why hire the brother too? I think the time is coming or is here when we need extra help around here just to make sure no one comes in and destroys anything. And two should go to town together. Now I don't trust anyone except the Andersons and I hope they don't get beat up cause of sticking with us."

"Glad our taxes are paying for that school," Linc sarcastically commented.

"Yeah, we pay taxes so they can tell us where our kids can be taught. That angers me to no end," Addy agreed.

"Another thing," Linc said, looking around at all at the table. "I think our days of shopping at Casson are at an end. Linksfort ain't that far, about 30 miles, while Casson is 10. Andersons go there a lot and I think we will have to too. Dan can tell us what stores to use and his people live there and that will be a big help. I don't think we will be shunned there. What about church here, Addy?"

"I'm done with that too," she answered. "Our good priest did not even say good morning the last time I went.

"We all know the Pattons give lots of money to that church and I suppose they can give the orders on who can get to heaven and not too. So that takes care of that."

"I want my baby baptized, Ma," Annie told her.

"How you gonna do that? We have to go where the

church boundary lines are set."

"There is a cathedral in Linksfort. They have to baptize. Or are supposed to," Linc told Annie.

"We'll have to check that out," Annie answered.

"Another thing," Addy told them. "I will never show mercy to anyone around here again except the Andersons. If I get the chance to hurt any of them, I will. I shall never respect anyone here, any of my neighbors, ever again!"

"Amen," Linc echoed.

"What if Ken and Pete tell someone about what you just said or what we talked about here today?" Annie asked.

"Don't worry about it. Who they gonna tell? The neighbors that won't even talk to us. I don't think you got to worry about that. We're an island here all by ourselves, isolated, alone. So we had better stick together."

That evening cut the final thread. Instead of Ruth waiting for him as he expected, Ted found her pa.

"I realize you are not at fault for your pa's problems, but I do feel I do not want to put any of them on my daughter's shoulders. We, her ma and I, feel it is better if she does not marry into your family."

"I couldn't agree more," Ted answered.

"Then you'll give us no trouble. That is sensible." Hesitating a moment, he added, "I feel it only fair to warn you, my brother Ray and I will do everything in our power to make sure none of the people in this town or in your neighborhood will have to put up with you people. We shall do everything in our power to remove you from this area."

"And how do you think you're gonna do that?" Ted asked.

"It shouldn't be too much of a problem. Your pa isn't capable of handling any of the financial affairs of your ranch anymore. I shall make sure that the town of Casson is aware of this. And my brother will make sure all your neighbors are also aware of this. Martin, being the sole owner of his ranch, is the only one that can buy or sell anything on his ranch. There is no way any ranch can continue without selling and buying and none of you can do that. And people, neighbors, businesses will not do business with a crazy man."

"And there you are wrong. All wrong!" Ted answered, his voice like a steel thread. "Addy and Linc own High Ranch. Bought it lock, stock and barrel. Pa does not own anything on it. Addy and I bought High Mile Ranch and everything on it, or half of it and the buildings. Pa's name is not on either ranch. Addy owns all of our River Ranch including all the machinery and the cattle, horses, everything. That was done a few years ago, not now, but a few years ago when Pa was real good. I've got a better idea. If you don't want us for neighbors, why don't you people move away. Sounds like a hell of a good idea."

Chapter II

"Addy, you get that letter written last night?" Ted asked the next morning.

"Yes, I did. Now it's got to be mailed somehow today."

"Linc and I talked this morning in the barn. We thought about you and me going to Adams and seeing those people. That teacher and her brother today. We could stop at Aunt Elsie's and find out where they live. If we think it's too far for one day, then we can probably stay overnight. What you think?"

"Can I leave so long with Martin like he is?"

"What difference does it make whether you're here or not. Pa does what he wants to and that way it would be taken care of," Ted answered.

"I was going to clean today, but guess that will keep until I get back. Yes, let's go and see what can be done. Sure hope it works out cause that would solve some problems. I can be ready in half an hour," Addy told Ted.

"Adams is not that far from Linksfort, is it?" Ted asked.

"About 10 miles on the other side. So that makes it about 40 miles from here. I think I'll take along my nightie just in case. Maybe we can stop at Linksfort on the way back and pick up some flour and groceries, like salt and we will need some kerosene for the lamps before long."

"Think of what you need on the way. Let's just get going now. If we leave soon, we should be there by noon."

"I'd better take along something for dinner. Ted, get a few eggs for me to take along too. And I'll take along some of the cookies I made yesterday. Sugar cookies are hard for Aunt Elsie to make with her rheumatism. And half of that coffee cake too."

On the drive to Adams, Ted asked Addy if she had any idea how to pay for the man and woman she hoped to hire.

"And where will they live?" he also added.

"I've been doing some book work and there is money there to pay them with. After we get back and when we have time, I think we all have to sit down and go over the figures."

"I think we had better do that right away, not put it off. Don't want to run short of money. Got to know where we're going cause I don't ever want to have to take back anything I said to old man Patton."

"You're right. As for where they will live? In my house, I suppose. I wanted them to come for more security and for teaching."

"You know the house on Big Mile Ranch ain't that far that they can't come down to our place every day. The buildings are only about a mile off the main road and it's about three miles from the main road to our buildings. With a horse that's not that far. And if they can drive a car, then it's not far at all. Then I won't worry about getting renters in there, like Linc has for his house on High Ranch."

"Wonder what kind of a house they are used to?" Addy asked.

"If they worked somewhere, probably not that fancy. A bunkhouse for him and boarding for her."

"That's true," Addy agreed. "Ted, what will Martin do this winter when he can't get outside? Or do you think he'll still try to walk every day, even in the drifts and cold?"

"Hard telling, Addy. Did Linc tell you Baldy's bridle is missing? I was going to ride her and couldn't find the bridle. And another horse bridle, one we use some of the time was laying in the water tank. It's those kind of things that rile Linc and me up. Just little things like tools laying around and missing and bridles laying here and there. And Pete and Ken say they don't do it."

"You don't suppose Martin is doing it?" Addy asked.

"You see him. He never takes anything when he leaves the buildings. Linc and I talked about that too and wondered, but we never see him take anything," Ted answered.

"But there are lots and lots of times when we don't see him, what he is doing. And especially at night. And he is gone lots of nights," Addy said.

"I don't know," Ted said, shrugging his shoulders.

"Nothing surprises me anymore, Ted. Just nothing. After yesterday, I'll believe anything. I didn't think I could take any more, but I found that I've got a whole new strength in me. I guess anger makes new energy and power."

"I hope our trip today isn't a wild goose chase," Ted added.

Noon found them at Aunt Elsie's. She was elated to have the unexpected company.

"Land's sake. So nice to have you here and you brought so many good things to eat. Cookies, and the roll out ones I can't make any more and fresh eggs too. Think I've got enough coffee for us and I made vegetable soup this morning, so we'll have plenty to eat. What with your coffee cake and cookies, we'll make out fine. Now what brings you here so unexpected?" she asked after getting them seated at the table.

"Aunt Elsie, you wrote in your last letter about the Parkers, I can't remember the woman's first name and I don't know which brother died. I remember one was called Tom, but can't remember the other one."

"Tom died. Stubby is the other one. His name was Harold, but he lost part of a finger as a child and the name Stubby stuck with him from then on. His sister was a teacher. Her name was Evie."

"Now I remember. Anyway, we wanted to talk to them and see if they needed jobs."

"I can see Stubby being a hired man, what with all the work you have there, but what would you want Evie for?"

"To teach Ken and Pete. I think I wrote that Martin wasn't feeling good. Well, that's only part of it," Addy told her aunt. "Martin has head problems. His mind seems to be going bad. He walks all the time and never washes himself and won't let me wash his clothes. He is bad tempered and can't talk very well. His words are blurred and we are all at a loss as to what is the matter."

"I've heard of those things happening," Aunt Elsie said.

"You have?" Ted asked.

"Oh yes. Several times. One lady I knew that had the same thing, was oddly enough Stubby and Evie's ma. And I hate to tell you this, but she got worse and worse until she did not know them at all. Oh yes, Addy, you think it is bad now, but it can get much worse. Evie's sister had to feed her and change the bed all the time and her clothes, diapered her in the end. She didn't even know any of the family."

"Oh Ted," Addy whimpered.

"Evie sent her sister money most every month, cause she was teaching and couldn't help her sister out. I think her sister hired some help and Evie paid for that. I think Stubby sent money too and so did Tom. That family helped each other out. The sister and her husband moved after the ma died, cause the neighbors were so nasty to them, they didn't want to stay there anymore. They didn't move when she was alive cause it would have been too hard to move the old lady."

Ted and Addy looked at each other. "Yes," Addy agreed, "we know what nasty neighbors are."

"A whole town that is nasty," Ted added.

"People can be real mean," Aunt Elsie agreed.

"What kind of a house do they live in now?" Ted asked. "Stubby and Evie, that is."

"I don't know. I have never seen it. But I wouldn't imagine it is very fancy. Cause she told me that the roof leaked in the last rain storm and the house will no doubt be cold in the wintertime. There is a shed or so because Stubby has some animals of some sort. You still haven't told me why you need a teacher?"

"Because I have been told my two boys can't go back to the school. They are not welcome. The school board will not be responsible for any problems or fighting that comes from their going back Tuesday. Sons of a crazy man aren't welcome."

"Nice people you have around you, Addy," Aunt Elsie commented. "And of course it would all be your two boys fault if fighting broke out?"

"According to the school board members that came to see me," Addy told her.

"All right. Help me with the dishes and I'll go with you to see the Parkers . It will be easier for me to go along than to try to direct you to where they live. You got somewhere for them to live, should they want to work for you?" she asked Ted.

"We have a house that no one is living in right now. Nothing fancy, but with soap and water and maybe a little paint, it could be livable."

"Better not offer that paint too soon. That can come later if everything works out all right," was the sage advice Aunt Elsie gave.

About two miles cross country, the three came upon a set of shack-like buildings setting on the prairie. Getting close, Addy could see the structures were tumbled down and hadn't had much for upkeep. They didn't have to worry about these people coming from a nice home. An older man come out of the house as soon as the car drove into the yard. Greeting Aunt Elsie, he looked several times at Addy, then his face creased in a smile as he greeted her.

"I remember you. You were Frank's wife. And this is..." he asked putting his hand out to Ted.

"This is Ted Rafferty, my stepson."

"Evie, see who is here," Stubby called to his sister as she came out of the house toward the car.

"I remember you," she told Addy. "And Elsie, how are you?" she asked giving the older woman a big hug. "Come on into the house."

"I wonder if I could have a drink of water?" Ted asked.

"Sure. It's warm. We have to carry our water here. Got some for the stock, but it ain't safe for us to drink. At least, I don't want to drink it. But there is a dipper and there is the ten gallon can. Help yourself," Stubby answered.

Inside the house both Addy and Ted were relieved to see it matched the outside. Looking down Addy could see the linoleum on the floor was clean, but very worn with the dark undercoating coming through here and there. Paper and wallpaper would have improved the walls, but from the looks of the furniture the money was not there to make this improvement. The inside was old, shabby, but very clean.

After a few minutes discussing the weather and general issues, Aunt Elsie, a forward no-nonsense person, told the two that there was a special reason Ted and Addy were visiting her that day.

"Special reason?" Evie asked.

"Yes," Addy answered. "I need a teacher for my two boys. Talking to Aunt Elsie this noon, I told her how my husband, Ted's pa, has been sick, and she said this sounded like how your ma was before she died, in her last years."

"I feel sorry for you if your husband is that way," Stubby told Addy.

"How sick is he now?" Evie asked. "I don't mean to put my nose where it don't belong, but I just wondered what he is doing that is not what he used to do."

Addy and Ted told them how Martin was compared to how he used to be. They nodded their heads occasionally, inserting little comments that told Ted and Addy that they knew what this sickness was.

"And how can we help you?" Stubby asked.

"I need a teacher because my children are not allowed to go into the school next Tuesday."

"People ought to be shot that do that to other people." Evie said. "My sister had it so hard with Ma and then the people were so nasty to them besides. Like it is catching or something. When Ma would run away the people would call her awful names. That hurt so."

"And we'd like to hire you for a hired man," Ted told Stubby. "Most of the neighbors, except one, are not talking to us. They avoid us. The people in Casson do too cause the local banker and his brother, one of our neighbors, have said they would drive us out of the area. The banker and his brother, Patton by name, hold loans on a lot of the ranches around us and businesses in town. They ain't gonna drive us away either cause the titles on the ranches are made out in such a way that they can't do what they would like to do. But we; Addy, Linc, my brother, and I; felt it would be better if we had another man on the place. One man to stay home while the other two went to town or wherever. We don't feel safe anymore," Ted explained.

"I don't know if anyone would actually hurt us. They won't talk to us, but I don't know if they would beat us up or anything, or set fire, or destroy anything. But we felt with so much hatred and mistrust around that we needed an extra man around. And I hoped that you would be able to help me a little in the house cause Martin is going to take more time, cause I do feel we will need to watch him more and more now," Addy added talking to Evie.

"Where would we live?" Stubby asked. "I have two cows I milk and a few range cows. Also a few chickens for eggs and to eat once in a while."

"There is a ranch we own about three to four miles from the home buildings. There is an old house on it. It needs a scrubbing right now, but it ain't too bad otherwise. And there are a few other buildings too. A small barn, a horse barn and a chicken coop, also a hog shed that could raise some hogs or sheep. Of course there would need to be a fence for them."

"And what pay would we get?" Stubby asked.

"Ted and I talked it over coming this morning. I didn't think to talk to Linc last night cause I was so mad, I just couldn't think too straight. So we just made up our minds this morning. We felt seventy-five cents a day for you, Stubby, and fifty cents a day for you, Evie. And you would have the buildings included as pay, rent free."

"I like the sounds of it. How about you Evie?" Stubby asked his sister.

"Yes. Sounds like something good. I can live with the neighbors not speaking to me. Don't bother me at all. And it sounds like there is room for your cows and chickens."

"The house has a kitchen, a parlor, two bedrooms downstairs and a large room upstairs that was never finished. Could be used for a storeroom," Ted told them, adding, "the kitchen has a pantry off of it and there even is a small room you come into before coming into the kitchen where barn clothes could be hung, at least in the summer. I don't think there are any closets, but I saw hooks on the walls in the bedrooms for clothes. There is a big kitchen stove that was left that works. I stayed there for a couple of weeks and used it to cook on. And they left an old round stove in the parlor, don't know if that works or not. They look pretty heavy, so I suppose that's why they were left. Maybe they thought them too heavy to move."

"That sounds good, Ted. Any garden spot?" Evie asked. "I would like to raise vegetables if I could. I can't here on this gumbo. Just won't raise anything, cause of grasshoppers and being so dry. Raises tumbling tumble weeds the best."

"You could have a garden spot down by us, down by the home buildings. We irrigate when we need to. Use a gasoline engine. Works pretty good too," Addy told her.

"How soon you want us to start?" Stubby asked.

"And where do I get the books for teaching?" Evie added.

"I'm hoping Jessie Anderson can get them for me from the school down by her that closed last May. I haven't talked to her yet, but I will when I get home. If I have to, I can go to the school the boys were supposed to go to and get them, but I won't if I can help it," Addy answered.

"Are those books still at that school?" Ted asked.

"The last I knew they were. The school board hadn't decided what to do with them yet. I guess they offered them to our school, but they didn't buy them, I hope they are still there. I imagine I can buy them for very little, I hope."

"Our rent is paid here until the 10th of September," Stubby told them. "By then we can be moved. I have to get hold of Perkins to move us. He has two trucks and he would be able to move everything at one time. Crate up the chickens and by stacking up the furniture too, we should be able to do it with his two trucks.

"He has cattle trucks?" Ted asked.

"Sure does," Stubby answered.

"Good. We're going to need trucks when we sell cattle. Casson don't think our money is any good anymore, so we'll need to find other businesses to deal with. Figure we'll have to go to Linksfort now. Farther, but maybe better in the long run," Ted said.

"Lester Perkins will treat you right and he won't be scared to come onto your ranch either, even if the other ranchers don't treat you right. He don't have to depend on them for his business, so he won't care. Say, ain't he related to some rancher in that area?" he asked his sister.

"Now that you mention it, yes. I think the name is Anderson."

"Dan Anderson?" Ted asked.

"I think so," was the answer.

"Sounds good," Addy said. "Maybe, just maybe, we'll make this thing through without many more problems."

The pleasure of solving some of the immediate problems was overshadowed by finding a new dilemma when they returned home. Ken and Pete had stumbled onto Martin's hideaway and he did not take kindly to their discovery.

The day Addy and Ted left, Annie had recruited Linc into helping her do a little fixing in a room for the coming baby. Ken and Pete, finding they had no work lined up for the afternoon, had taken their horses and gone riding. To Shep's joy they followed the river bottoms, exploring a portion of the river not disturbed by man or cattle. Firewood in the winter was cut from easier accessible places and the cattle drank where the river banks were not so steep.

"Oh look Pete," Ken said. "That's where the boards, planks, and timbers from the bridge went when it got washed out a couple of years ago. Let's crawl down the bank and look at it."

"Sure," Pete agreed. Intent on watching, so they did not fall, they scampered down the bank. They did not notice Martin until Pete felt a blow from a large stick across his back. The blow knocked him down the hill. Lumbering after him, Martin swung again and again hitting the boy anywhere from the shoulders to his legs.

Ken tried in vain to get the stick away from Martin. Only Shep's frantic barking seemed to penetrate Martin's desire to eliminate the intruder. Swinging around, he started after the dog, only to shift his attention to Ken. Well aimed blows on the boy's shoulders and body hurt, but one blow grazed his head, rendered the boy senseless for a few moments. Recovering, he stumbled and lost his balance. He rolled down the steep bank into the river below. The shallow water seemed to revive him and he staggered down the riverbed until he could find a place to crawl up the bank. Martin watched him go, then walked around and around in a circle finally assuring himself that he had eliminated the trespassers. Throwing the stick down, he walked back toward the pile of old rotting lumber.

Watching from a patch of blackberry briers where he had hidden, Pete waited until he was sure his pa had gone. Satisfied, he left the hiding place and carefully made his way toward Ken. Very quietly the boys went to where they had tied the horses. Finding they were both so badly beaten they could not ride, they walked home leading their horses.

"Oh, that looks fine," Annie told Linc when they had finished working on the baby room. "I'll make supper quick. Wonder where Ken and Pete are?"

"They should be home by now," Linc answered. "They know they got to be home or they'll go without supper. Damn it, seems like they got to be in trouble all the time. First with taking the tools and then lying. Bad enough with Pa always on our minds. They should know better than try to pull anything. Got enough to do and think about without them making more problems."

"Well, if they ain't here, we'll eat without them." Busy putting on the supper, Annie happened to glance out the kitchen window. "There they are coming home, but why are they walking? Both of them, way in the distance."

"Guess we'll know when they get here," Linc answered.

"You and Ted ever do things like that, get into trouble?" Annie asked.

"We sure never took tools without asking and sure put them back when we were done. Pa would have taken a stick to us good if we hadn't," he answered. "You don't need to go to the door. They'll know where supper is," Linc admonished her as she went out the door.

"Linc, they are walking so funny. Oh my goodness!" she shouted as they got closer. "Linc they are hurt, both of them. What happened?" she called.

"Pa beat us up," Pete answered.

"Linc, come here," Annie called. "Please!"

"Pa beat us up with a big stick," Ken told Linc as he came closer.

"Hell and damnation," Linc exclaimed running his hands over them. "What happened?"

"We followed the river bank until we came to that big pile of boards and timbers and planks that got piled up when the bridge went out a couple of years ago," Ken said. "So we went to see what it looked like. We never saw Pa until he started to beat on Pete."

"He hit me with a stick."

"Big one," Ken interrupted. "I tried to take it away from him, only Pa's bigger than me. I think he heard Shep bark, cause he don't like Shep anymore. I saw him kick him good one day and since then Shep don't go by him. Anyway, he started to go after Shep and then he saw me and started to hit me with the stick."

"He hit Ken on the head and I thought he was dead. I watched and Ken started to roll and rolled down the river-bank into the river. He went down the river until the bank wasn't so steep and he could get out. Pa never went after him."

"Where were you when Pa was hitting Ken?" Linc asked.

"I hid behind some blackberries. Pa looked around and around and walked around and around in a little circle and then threw the stick and went back down by the rotten boards. I went by Ken, when I knew Pa was gone, and we went to the horses."

"Only we couldn't ride them cause we hurt so much. My butt hurts awful," Ken told them.

"Linc, I see your pa coming," Annie said.

"I'll run up to the house and get clean clothes for the boys before he gets here. You clean them up down here," he told her.

Taking warm water out of the stove reservoir, Annie began washing the dirt out of the cuts and bruises.

"You boys sure are going to be sore for a few days until these heal. One of you is in just as bad of shape as the other. I wish Linc would bring those clean clothes for you. And I don't have enough iodine to put on where the skin is broken. Linc figured he'd get back here before your pa got home."

But Linc had his hands full with a still angry Martin.

"Why Pa, why did you hit Ken and Pete like you did?" he asked.

But Martin did not answer. Linc watched him swear and stumble around the kitchen, not seeming to grasp what he was asked. Linc finally understood his pa did not know who Pete and Ken were and he wondered if Martin even knew who he was. Realizing after he picked up a kitchen chair, that he intended to smash it against the kitchen door, Linc struggled until he finally got the chair away from the older man.

"My place, my place," Linc was finally able to understand. "Leave me be." With this Martin went out the door and walked back toward the barn and back to the riverbottoms.

"Linc," Annie called as she heard him come into their house.

"Yeah, Pa went back to the river. How the boys look?" he asked.

"Bad. Your ma has a big bottle of iodine up there. You'll have to get it cause I don't have enough."

"We got to have that stuff put on us?" Ken asked. "Ain't it enough that we got beat up, without having to have that stinging stuff on us too?"

"We'll blow," Annie told him. "Then you boys can lay down for awhile, while I make supper. Here or in your beds."

"Here," Pete answered.

"I'll have to lay a quilt on the floor cause I have only one bed," Annie said.

"Here on the floor," Pete answered. "I'm scared to go back up there even if Pa has gone back to the river."

After chores were done and the evening had settled in, the four talked about sleeping arrangements for the night.

"We'll sleep at the big house tonight. Ted is gone and we'll use his bed. I don't want the boys there alone with Pa when he comes back. I know he never touched them before, but I would just feel better if we stayed there," Linc told Annie.

"I don't want to stay there with him alone," Pete said.

"Me either," Ken echoed.

"You boys don't know why Pa protected that place do you? You didn't see what was there?" Linc asked.

"No. We never got the chance."

"After Ted gets back and Pa is sleeping in the early morning, we'll go down there and see."

"I don't want you to go alone," Annie told him.

"No. It would be foolish to go alone. Pa has a lot of strength. Maybe his mind is going, but he is still strong as a bull. I had all I could do to take that chair away from him."

"Ma will be just sick," Annie said.

"And she has a right to be. More problems." Linc answered.

The following evening the family, excluding Martin, sat on the porch steps discussing the preceding two days. The boys sat close to Addy, one on each side. Occasionally, she squeezed their hands.

"You got to quit crying, Ma," Ken said.

"It hurts me so to see you look like you do," she answered. "And it hurts even more to know your pa did this to you. He's sick in the head or he wouldn't have done this. A couple of years ago if this had happened to anyone and he heard of it, he would have been so angry. He was always so gentle, kind, good, firm, but good. And now...just look at you."

"We had two good days. Got our schoolteacher and a hired man. Good one, I think. And made some stops in Linksfort, talked to a cattle trucker and a lawyer. Also changed our post office to there."

"Got to go into Casson yet for that though?" Linc asked.

"No, dropped a letter to the Casson post office from there and took care of it. Anderson's uncle is postmaster there."

"That sounds like a good town," Annie said.

"It will be good. The Patton's don't have nothin' to say there. And don't carry any weight either. Nice to know. Just wish it weren't so far," Ted answered.

"You gonna help them clean up that house?" Linc asked Addy.

"No, they're gonna set up beds and Evie will clean up a room at a time. It don't seem to bother her to do it that way. Said she would rather, than have me try to get it done for her. She's a clean woman. That house will be clean. I think the pay and a roof over their heads..."

"Free roof," Ted interrupted.

"Yes, free roof," Addy agreed. "I think that made all the difference in the world. She said I shouldn't worry about it. The books for Ken and Pete have to be found yet. The school board here didn't have the money to pay for those books from that school. Course, maybe they didn't think they needed them that bad either. Anyway, I'm going to see Jessie tomorrow and see if I can get them. It may be several weeks before Evie can start to teach, but that's all right. By that time she'll be done cleaning."

"You gonna get some paint?" Annie asked.

"I'll see how bad it looks first. Maybe wait until spring. No sense in getting it painted and then they don't work out."

"That makes good sense," Linc told her.

"You notice the soles on Stubby's shoes?" Ted asked Addy.

"No. But I saw that Evie's had holes in them and I could see cardboard through the holes. I think she noticed that I saw and she sat real straight on her chair."

"Stubby had cardboard soles in his shoes too. I think they are mighty happy to have a place to go. If all they had to live on was the eggs from those hens, a few cattle to sell, and the little jobs that he could pick up here and there, makes mighty poor living," Ted added.

"You boys should go to bed," she told Ken and Pete. "Hard to sleep?"

"I laid on my stomach so it wouldn't hurt where I was hit," Ken replied.

"Same here," Pete echoed.

"Wait here," Addy told the others, as she went with Ken and Pete on their way to bed. "I want to talk to all of you." In a few minutes she was back.

"You think Pa will try to hit them again here in the house or on the yard?" she asked Linc.

"I don't know," he slowly answered. "I just don't know.

Pa can't hardly talk, can't understand him. Guess that's why he don't talk at all now. And he's angry so much of the time. I just don't know."

"There's something here that scares me," Annie said. "When will Martin turn on Ma and do the same to her that he did to those boys? He comes home whenever he feels like it. Sleeps on the floor, but what happens if suddenly he gets mad at Ma and takes a stick or who knows what when she is sleeping in bed. If he would, he could kill her before anyone could get there to defend her."

"I thought of that too," Linc said.

"I've thought of nothing else since we got home," Ted said." I sleep upstairs so I don't hear him come home at all."

"Addy, use that small room that you use for sewing and storage off the kitchen to sleep in. There is that bed upstairs that nobody uses. Move that down there and sleep in there. That's close to your bedroom."

"I wonder if Pa would notice if his bedroom were locked after he goes in there? We could put a lock on it. Buy one in Linksfort," Ted said.

"Good idea," Linc agreed.

"I know Addy, but Pa ain't Pa anymore," Linc told her as she started to cry.

"It is taking away his dignity," she said.

"When he was Pa, yes. Now, he's not Pa anymore and I'm afraid of your being hurt and of the rest of us too. I sure don't want him to hit Annie," Linc said.

"And from what Aunt Elsie said, it probably will get worse," Ted said.

"Worse? How?" Annie asked.

"Stubby's and Evie's Ma had the same thing. And she finally got so she had to be fed and diapered like a child. She didn't know anyone," Annie answered.

"I wonder if that wouldn't be better than this," Linc said. "At least we would know where he was and he couldn't hurt anyone."

"A day at a time. We'll just have to live it a day at a time," Addy said.

Chapter III

The ranch settled down to an uneasy existence. Several days after Martin's fiasco with Ken and Pete, Ted and Linc, very early in the morning, rode along the river bottoms until they came to Martin's hideout.

"That must be it," Ted told Linc as they came up to the boards and timbers piled along the bank. "It's still plenty dark, but I guess we can see what it looks like."

"Look at this," Linc said. "Just look at this. Pa made some sort of a room here. These boards are nailed together to make this."

"What size you suppose this is? About five feet wide? And it must be at least four feet tall."

"Have to crawl in," Linc said, getting down on hands and knees to get into the room. "Pa put a lot of effort into this. And a lot of the nails from the farm."

"And here is the hammer we accused the boys of losing. And the pail of nails we looked for and couldn't find. And here is one of our saws and a pliers. Here's the broken one, but here is the better one."

"And Addy's kettle she looked high and low for and

another pan and a lid too. And matches, lots of them. Those we're taking back with us. If Pa started a fire in this woods, and the wind was right, he could burn up a lot of woods. It's so dry outside."

"Yeah, including the buildings, if it got out of hand enough," Ted agreed. "Wonder what he wanted these for?"

"What you looking at?" Linc asked.

"Old rags and pants and stuff Addy uses for making rugs. A whole sack of them, just like Addy packed them away for working with during the winter. He must have just taken the whole works."

"Here are some more tools and here are some of our traps. We would have looked high and low for them this winter when we wanted to start trapping." Linc held up several to show Ted. "We owe an apology to our brothers."

"We sure do," he agreed. "We sure do. Who would have thought it would come to this. If anyone would have told me this several years ago, I would have punched them in the face. Our pa should come to this. I can't hardly believe it, even when I see it day after day."

"I think we'd better get back. We got all the chores to do yet. I think I got all the matches. Let's make sure we got them all." Ted helped him look again and when they didn't find anymore, they left the hideout, climbing up the bank toward their horses.

"Looks like we've got another to milk," Ted remarked when they came in sight of the barn. "That heifer must have had her calf."

"Been better if she would have had it six months from now when the other cow was dry so we would have milk for the houses all the time. You know when winter sets in and when Pa can't get back there anymore, we'll have to go back and get everything."

"Yeah, that we will. We never looked under those sacks of rags, but we are still missing one bridle. I wonder if it is back there?" Ted asked.

"Either there or along the way if he dropped it. Not going back now to check it out. I see Pa coming now. He's early this morning. Damn glad we got out of there when we did." Ted agreed.

The boy's bruises and cuts healed. But they always carried with them a fear of their pa. Knowing how gentle he had been before his sickness, this hurt Addy so much. Both Ted and Linc apologized to the youngsters for the injustice done to them when they had been accused of misplacing and stealing from the shop and harness room.

Addy never slept in the same room with Martin again. The small storage and sewing room off the kitchen was cleaned out and a bed moved in. From then on, Addy slept there. Martin continued to sleep on the rug on the floor, but never once did he seem to miss Addy. After crying a few tears over this, Addy accepted that he would never be the old Martin again.

A month later, Linc and Annie made a trip to Linksfort to get flannel for diapers and baby clothes.

"Don't forget to buy a lock for the bedroom door," Addy reminded them as they were leaving.

"I won't," Linc assured her. "Got to go to the feed mill and see where we can get wheat ground for flour and also the banker."

"And Lester Perkins too," Ted reminded him. "Those cattle are ready to be sold now."

"You remember the name of the banker?" Annie asked Linc as he got into the car.

"Sure, Dave Lay."

"So glad for the Andersons, Jessie and Dan. They are true friends," Addy said, "Make it good now."

"I hope they will have time to go to the Cathedral too," Ted told her as they watched the car going down the driveway.

Linc and Annie's trip to Linksfort set further groundwork for future business relations. A visit to the mill assured them they would have their flour supply for the winter, plus a supplier of cotton cake and block salt for the cattle. Linc found Dan Anderson had already mentioned the Rafferty's to Dave Lay, the banker, so the reception there was warm. With the sale of cattle, some money would be put in the bank so some of the bills could be paid with check.

Before the sun had hardly started to rise the following Tuesday morning, Lester Perkins' two trucks had made the trip to the Rafferty's, loaded the cattle and were on their way to the Linksfort sale barn.

Knowing she could not invite them in for breakfast, Addy took freshly baked baking powder biscuits, jelly and coffee out to the trucks for the men to eat before they started back on the road.

"I would have liked to had them in to eat in the house," she told Linc as the trucks started down the driveway.

"That's all right, Addy. They are in a hurry anyway. Got a lot of trucking for all day, they told me. The coffee and biscuits went fast for them and I know they appreciated it."

"Seem to be nice men, both of them. I thought that when they brought Stubby and Evie's things."

"They are," Linc agreed.

"How much do they know about Martin?" Addy asked.

"A little. Stubby told them that the old man here was getting sick in the head, like his ma was before she died. And Lester told Stubby that it does happen, but it would make no difference as long as we could pay for the trucking. And Stubby told him that we would. He said he didn't know how it was made out, but sounded to him like the money was not in the old man's hands anymore. Stubby said he didn't want to say too much, but enough so when they came for trucking, if they saw Pa they wouldn't think it funny Pa didn't say anything."

"Ted said he mentioned it to the lawyer, Talor, but didn't say anything at the post office. None of their business."

"That town will be different from Casson for us, Addy," Linc told her. "I got the impression from Lay when I was in the bank and talked to him that he didn't care much for Pattons, neither one. Just the way he acted. Didn't say anything bad about either of them, but the feeling was there that he didn't like them. He said he handled business dealings different than they did and from that I got the idea he didn't think much of them."

"The feeling is one I share," Addy told him. "I better get dishes done before Jessie and Dan come. The school books are coming this morning. I don't think Pete or Ken are excited about it, but when Evie gets done scrubbing, and maybe even before, the learning starts again."

"You lucked out on those books. Getting them for nothing. Couldn't believe it."

"I was surprised, but glad. I think Jessie and Dan had a lot to do with that. But according to them, they had to get rid of them somehow. With the school closing and a family moving into the schoolhouse to live, it was one less thing for them to worry about getting rid of."

"And for once it worked out for us," Linc told her. "Stubby and Evie seem to be working out for us too."

"Two things," Addy agreed. "But the biggest heartache is sleeping in the house now." And Linc had to agree with her.

Hardly had Addy gotten her dishes done before the Andersons drove in with their car full of school books, crayons, chalk and even a small blackboard.

"You are a blessing," Addy told them as she helped carry in the boxes.

"Glad to help," Dan told her. "I think one more load will do it."

"And while you are getting it, I'll get out cups and coffee and we'll have baking powder biscuits. I baked them this morning so I could give Perkins and his driver some before they left here this morning."

"They here for cattle?" Dan asked.

"Yes. Took two loads. Ted and Stubby went after them to take care of the money."

"How do you think you're going to like Linksfort?" Dan asked as he took his first bite of the biscuit covered with jelly.

"Good. Both Linc and Ted are satisfied. Oh, it's not like

going into Casson. That was like going home, that is until now. Now, it's hell."

"That's because of the Pattons. I thought the bank was the only place holding mortgages, but I think Darwins owe lots of money to Ray and I know Boyens and Clarks do. Henry Martin and Clinton told me that the other day. That is the reason why they go along with whatever Ray Patton says. Ray holds their mortgages. He told them if they were even a little friendly with you people, he would call in their mortgage. And the bank holds mortgages on so many of the businesses in town that they are doing the same thing cause they are afraid of the bank."

"Nice people," Jessie said, putting jelly on her biscuit. "These are good, Addy. You always were a good cook."

"Thank you. Dan, what do the Pattons hope to get done by doing this to us."

"Put you out of business and get your ranches."

"They can't do that."

"No. But they put it around that Martin can't do business anymore cause he's nuts and no body else can sell anything or do anything. Now with you doing business in Linksfort and having cash and being able to sell anything you want to, well it kind of makes liars out of them."

"A few years ago Martin had everything here sold to me. He sold it to me, the ranch and the cattle and the machinery, just everything. He did it so his sister couldn't get her hands on anything after he died. And so I own everything here. And High Ranch, Linc and I bought with money I inherited, and Ted and I bought part of Big Mile Ranch the same way. I put my money into it and we both signed the deed. There ain't no way they can touch us, unless our cattle get sick or a fire or something like that."

"But the Pattons didn't know this. And old man Johnson was your lawyer?" Dan asked Addy.

"Yes."

"And he's dead."

"He died right after this was all done. After Martin sold all this to me."

"And so no one told Pattons all of this. Nothing goes on in Cassville that they don't know about. Just nothing cause they have their fingers, or rather the money in everything. That's what I didn't like about doing business there. You didn't do anythingwithout them knowing about it right away."

"Ted and Linc think Pattons don't have much to say about anything in Linksfort," Addy told Dan.

"No. Dave Lay and Joe and Ray Patton went to school together, college that is, and Lay said then Joe Patton was a cheat. He didn't mind who he cheated. You had to watch him all the time. But Ray Patton is the one with the brains. Not so much Joe. Ray has the brains."

"All right, Dan. Answer me this. If it wasn't for Ray Patton and his holding mortgages for Boyens and Clarks, would they treat us different? Charles Boyens always did think he was better than anyone else and Herman Clark is such a different person. I never could feel that he was easy to talk to or get to know even after all this time. Martin used to say that he was a loner, liked to be alone."

"I do know that they, some of them, have a great fear of Martin's craziness and don't want to have any of it rub off on them. And I know some of them are glad Ken and Pete are not in school."

"That's pure foolishness," Jessie said, anger in her voice.

"But true," Dan told her. "Sad to say, that's the way it is."

"Do any of them not speak to you because you befriend us?" Addy asked.

"I never was on the best of terms with any of them cause we, Jessie and me, have our family at Linksfort and we always went there to shop and to church. So we never did have much to do with anyone here and now I sure am glad."

"They certainly don't worry about you and Martin or your family," Jessie told Addy.

"Oh yes they do," Addy disagreed. "They worry plenty. On how to get rid of us!"

"You used to go to church so much," Jessie said to Addy.

"Do you now? I know it isn't any of my business, but we wondered about that."

"I haven't been to church for a long time: Ever since our good priest didn't even give me the time of day. He turned his back on me when I came out the door and spoke to someone else. That is the last time I went to church. I think Pattons give a lot to church and so I guess that gives them the say so of who gets to heaven and who doesn't."

"We wondered about that," Jessie said, giving Dan a quick look.

"Linc and Annie talked to someone at the Cathedral in Linksfort when they were there a week ago. That priest said he would have to check with the Bishop and see if their baby could be baptized or not. Annie should have the baby about Thanksgiving time. Maybe by then someone will have made up their mind."

"Gives one a bad taste in the mouth," Dan said.

"Gives me a bitter taste, one I won't forget soon, if ever. I know I will never go out of my way to do anything for anyone around here again. I used to take food to those that were sick. Martin would go with me and we would visit them when they were sick or had problems. Never again. I told Linc I would like to learn to drive, but now I don't know if I should cause I couldn't ever go alone or with Annie alone. We are afraid to goout alone now."

"You think someone would hurt you?" Jessie asked.

"We don't know, but no one goes anywhere alone now. Always two men or two people together and one man is always around here somewhere. We just don't know if anyone would come in here and do anything or not," Annie answered.

"Makes me sick," Dan told her. "Just makes me sick. Oh, by the way, our nice school board does know you have a teacher hired and that you have books. I don't know who told them, but I got asked about it yesterday."

"And how does our good school board like that?" Addy asked.

"Fine, I guess. Just as long as Ken and Pete don't show

up at school they really don't care. They really don't. We've got to go home Jessie," Dan said as he started walking to the door.

"As long as the boys don't have to start school with Evie until the first of the month, Linc and I thought it would be a good time to get their help and brand the calves. They can be good help, both sure know how to ride," Ted told Addy at breakfast the next morning.

"It would be one less thing to do later, but ain't it a little early cause of flies?"

"We'll coat the skin where the brand is with linseed oil. Stubby said that was how they always did it when he worked for some of the other ranches. It helps heal the wound and keeps flies and worms out of the raw area," he answered.

"Your pa always did it later cause then the cattle were down here and it was close to the buildings and easier he thought," Addy said.

"I know, but we're going to try it this way this year."

"How soon you starting?" Addy asked.

"In a couple of days. Got a few things to finish up here and then we have to check the fence and corral by the buildings on High Ranch and also Big Mile Ranch. Think we'll camp out at Evie and Stubby's. Just take along horse hide robes and sleep in the hay barn in the hay and straw. Ken and Pete can't wait. I told them about it this morning and they think that will be a big adventure."

"Sure. They have always been in school when this was done except on weekends and then they didn't get to sleep in a barn on the hay. I'll talk to Evie and we'll have to work out something for food," Addy answered.

Two days later the two boys, Ted and Stubby left to brand calves. As someone had to stay home Linc said he would. Not only were there chores to do on the home place, but there was always the underlining fear of someone in the neighborhood making trouble and problems for the family.

The first day the two boys and the two men spent rounding up the cattle. By luck the second head count showed the same amount of brood cows taken up in the spring. Driving them into a smaller pasture, they were able to keep them in one place for the night. By dark they were at Evie's eating the supper she and Addy had planned. A few minutes to relax after the hot meal and they all were ready to sleep under the horse robes Stubby had brought back with him the night before.

Although neither boy expected to go to sleep right away, within a few minutes they were dead to the world. Ted smiled at their excitement and then slowly drifted to sleep too.

It took several minutes of early morning crowing from the roosters Stubby had before the three came awake the next morning. In a few minutes they were coming into Evie's kitchen to smell the coffee brewing on the stove and pancakes frying on the hot griddle.

"You can have a half cup of coffee each," Ted told Ken and Pete. "Just fill the rest of the cup up with milk."

"Gee, just like a man," Pete said, watching as Evie poured the steamy, strong, hot liquid into the cup before him.

"Work like a man, then you can drink coffee just like a man," Ted told him. "But only a half cup. Evie, I think I'm getting too old to ride like we did yesterday and then sleep in a barn."

"Well, you're not their age anymore," she answered, nodding her head to Ken and Pete.

"No, guess I'm not. You've got lunch packed for us today?" he asked.

"Yes. Stubby is here now so as soon as he eats I suppose you can be on your way. Ready to brand them and get it done?"

"Yes. We'll get them done today and then tomorrow we'll work over here. Got a few at the home ranch to do too before we're done. Morning Stubby. As soon as you're done eating we can go."

Taking along the lunch Evie had packed they soon were on their way. By ten they had the fire going. Amongst the bellowing and calling of the brood cows and bawling of the calves, they got the calves separated from their mothers. Soon the stench of burning hair and hide penetrated the air. As each calf was branded, a good coating of linseed oil was run over the open wound. A short break at noon and then they resumed their job, finishing shortly before the middle of the afternoon.

"We'll keep them here in this pasture for a week or so," Ted told Stubby when they were done. "Be easier to watch them and keep an eye out for any sick ones."

"That sounds like a smart thing to do. They got water here and some grass too, so they'll be all right for a few days here. Let's go back home and see if Evie has any hot water so we can take a sponge bath. Like to crawl into a big tub of water, but guess that's not to be done," Stubby said.

"Could go by the dam. I don't know how cold that water would be, but we could all take a dunking in there," Ted suggested.

"Let's just go see how cold it really is," Stubby answered, heading his horse in that direction.

"You going to see how cold it is first?" Stubby asked as he watched Ted start to take off his clothes when they came to the water.

"Hell, no. I'm just going in and get this dust off of me," Ted answered.

"Well,come on boys, if he can do it so can we," Stubby said, starting to shed his clothes too.

"We don't have anything to dry ourselves off with, but I sure feel better," Stubby said as he started to dress after they left the water. "Getting all that dust and hair off of a person sure helps. Now let's go home and see what Evie has cooking on the stove."

The next day they worked the hills and the prairie at Big Mile Ranch and the following day they branded those calves. Before Ted and the two boys left for home that afternoon, they drove over in Stubby's car to check the calves they had branded several days before at High Ranch.

"Looks good," Ted said as they drove among them. "Can't see any with infection yet. Have to come back again in a couple of days and check them again. OK, let's go back, Stubby. Me and the boys are going to go home where we can sleep in a bed again."

"Maybe you didn't like where we slept, but we thought it was great," Ken said to Ted. "I wonder if Ma would let us sleep in our hay barn at home if we asked her."

"Don't know. Only way you'll ever know is to ask. I thought by now you'd be glad to have a good bed to sleep in," Ted answered.

"We slept on straw in the barn and when we get home we'll sleep on a straw mattress. So what's the difference?" Pete asked.

"Guess you've got something there," Ted answered laughing. "Maybe not much difference except the roosters are farther away in the morning."

The first part of October, school began for Pete and Ken. The home tutoring the boys were getting was excellent as Evie proved to be a very good teacher. She allowed no shirking, the work was done well and they progressed very nicely. When Addy could see how well it was going, she hoped Evie was in no hurry to quit her job. Although Ken had only two years to go to be out of eighth grade, Pete had four. The arrangement seemed to suit them all. Evie was happy because of the house she now lived in and the extra money coming in. She had always enjoyed teaching. Addy knew Ken and Pete were learning far more than they would have had they continued in the country school. Even Ken and Pete seemed to enjoy the home tutoring.

"I want to know where the money is coming from and what we have to buy," Ted had said many weeks before this, right after his final talk with Joe Patton. And so several weeks after the first load of cattle went to Linksfort, the family sat down to talk about their financial situation.

Addy took the bookkeeping ledgers out so the men could acquaint themselves with the system. Even Annie took part in the venture as Addy had asked her to be present.

"I've been doing it, writing everything down, but I don't like the job and I feel I don't have the time. I got to do it when it is late at night and I'm tired and it is hard to keep my eyes open then and my mind right. Annie was always good at figures in school, so I thought maybe she could learn how to do it, with you men keeping an eye on everything so it is right," Addy told all of them that morning. After many hours of going over everything, and by being very frugal, they knew there was money for the bills, the taxes and for general living expenses.

"And so we keep fifty dollars in the bank at Linksfort at all times and the rest here at home?" Annie asked.

"Yeah. When we have to write a check, then we put back enough to keep that amount there. The rest we keep in coffee cans, hidden here and there on the ranch here."

"I hope we remember where we got it all stacked away," Addy told them.

"We will," Linc assured her.

"I don't feel right coming back the same time and on the same road on Tuesday anymore either," Ted said. "There are so many men not working now that the auction barn is full.

"They ain't got nothing better to do so they come there and sit and visit and watch. And now our name is getting known and it looks like we got money when we are selling. Stubby and I talked about it last week and we decided to come back a different time and on a different road too. Stubby is taking along his shotgun every time now too."

"Don't you go and get shot," Addy said, "We don't need that."

"No, I don't intend to, but I don't intend to get held up either."

"It's a good idea to go a different way and at a different time," Linc agreed.

"Dan Anderson sells some of his steers to the meat

market there. I wonder if that could be another place to sell. Maybe a different day too."

"Would it pay for Perkins to come here for a couple of animals. Pay for the trucking?" Annie asked.

"Perkins has an old truck he asked if we wanted to buy. It runs good, but it don't look good cause it's been rolled over. He has it sitting at home. We can have it for $25.00."

"He got three trucks?" Addy asked.

"Yeah. Only now he says two trucks is enough so he is going to sell the smaller one. Anyway, it needs work on it that we could do. Bend it out some and it would be real usable for us. It would be nice for hauling wheat to the mill for our winter's flour and also getting block salt and cotton cake."

"Then cash the check and buy it next week when you go. You can follow each other home," Linc said.

"That will really confuse everybody when we head out of town a different direction," Ted said. "Yeah, a truck would be nice here. And we would have the money for it. Maybe get him to throw in that forge and anvil he has there. He said he was needing a better one. That sure would be good enough for us. Stubby said if we had one here he would make us a snowplow out of lumber and scrap medal we have. But he would need to weld it together in places to make it hold. A snowplow would be nicer than using the old drag piled with heavy stones for plowing snow."

"For nothing, you'll buy it, the anvil and forge?" Addy asked.

"Maybe he'll throw it in free," Ted laughed as he answered her.

It didn't go exactly like that, but for a small charge Ted acquired the anvil and forge for the ranch shop. After a few weeks, they wondered how they had gotten along without it before, especially now when they had been forced to take all their welding to Linksfort and not Casson.

Neither Linc nor Ted knew anything about using the new tools, but many years before, Stubby had worked with a blacksmith and the skills he had learned then were soon put to work. The snow plow was made for the long snowy winter months coming, along with repairing many other items on the ranch.

The day before Halloween Linc woke Addy to tell her that Annie was in labor and they were on their way to the hospital at Linksfort.

"Make it good," Addy told them both of them before they left.

"Ma, pray for me," Annie asked.

"I'll have to get some religion back," she answered her daughter, giving her a final hug before closing the car door. Shivering, she went back into the house to stand by the window looking out into the night. Moonlight illuminated the yard. Addy watched one of the barn cats going across the yard toward the river. She supposed the cat was hoping to catch a mouse or two for it's nightly meal. Knowing she wouldn't sleep even if she laid down, she finally dressed and went outside, walking toward the corral. She stood a few minutes looking at the horses. Baldy, always affectionate by nature, came to get petted.

What a difference a year makes, she thought. A year ago everything was so nice. I would have been sleeping beside Martin. Now he sleeps on the floor and I sleep in another room on a small bed. I keep his door locked at night. A year ago we talked everything out, never had any secrets from each other. And now I can't talk to him at all cause he don't seem to even know who I am or care that I'm his wife. A year ago we could go into Casson anytime and find friends to visit with along the streets or in the stores. Now we go to Linksfort cause we're not welcome in Casson. A year ago we would have been already thinking about Christmas and school and how much we looked forward to the visiting and the program. Now the boys are getting taught here at home cause they can't go to that school, even if our taxes are helping pay for it. A year ago I went to church every chance I could and now I don't go at all. And I quit praying cause I don't feel like it anymore. And a year ago, Martin never walked any further than to get on his horse and now the horse gets rode by someone else cause he only walks. I should be happy cause I'm gonna be a grandma and I guess I am happy. Wouldn't it be an awful thing if that baby would die or even worse, not be right. What a punishment that would be. Course I don't know what we got to be punished for. We didn't do anything wrong. Feeling tears starting to well in her eyes, Addy laid her head against the wooden cornerpost of the corral and wept.

Toward evening, the following day, Linc came home with the news of a healthy baby daughter.

"I never knew babies took so long to be born. What an awful waiting room," he told Addy. "We got there about midnight and the baby wasn't born until two this afternoon. Annie looked all worn out. Glad they make them stay in bed for ten days cause she'll need that to rest up."

"You got a name for my new niece?" Ken asked.

"That's right. You are an uncle now, ain't you?" Linc answered. "Yes. Her name is Sara Anne. Annie just liked the name Sara and I thought Anne sounded right with it. And Addy," Linc said, "I went over to the Cathedral before I came home and we can't get the baby baptized there. So I guess she won't get baptized at all."

"Well, I guess that's that then. Ray Patton and Joe Patton can sit in church every Sunday and call themselves Christians. I call it nothing but meanness and greed. It ain't right, but so be it," Addy answered as she angrily slammed a frying pan on top of the black cookstove.

The first blizzard of the winter came the first day of December, followed by a Chinook wind that melted the drifts. A week later another heavy snow covered the prairie and ranch with whiteness. Sunny skies followed putting a shimmering shine over the entire area.

"It's really hard to keep my eyes wide open. It is so glaring out there," Ted told Addy at noon. "Stubby is giving that snowplow a workout. He's got our driveway plowed out and he's even got it open to the main road and all the way up to where we feed cattle in the pasture. He wanted to open the driveway to Big Mile Ranch on his way home today."

"Shucks. Then Evie will be here tomorrow and we'll have to have school again," Ken said.

"Glad you don't have to study today," Ted told him. "We got plenty of work for you to do."

"You got plenty of work for Stubby too, don't you," Addy asked Ted.

"Plenty. With Pa not doing anything now, someone had to pick up what he used to do. I see Pa is walking back and forth on the driveway and where Stubby plowed or where we shoveled between the barns and the corral."

"I see that. I watched what he would do too," Addy answered. "Ken, Pete and I took down his bed this morning and put it upstairs. We laid the mattress on the floor. I made it up as best I could. I'm hoping he'll lay down on that now. The floor is so cold even with all his clothes on. I threw quilts on the top, hoping he'll cover with them. I don't know if he will or not. I hid all his summer clothes. He prowled around the room looking and looking for them this morning and finally put on the warmer shirts and even the long underwear."

"How do you know he put on the underwear?" Ted asked.

"Cause he was going to go outside in only them. I finally got him to put on the overalls."

"That must have been a challenge," Ted said.

"I started to put them on myself to show him how and he took them away from me and put them on. He still knew enough that he knew they were his."

"He put them on just so you wouldn't?" Ted asked.

"He did not want me to put them on," Addy quietly answered. "He put them on and that is what I wanted. Shoes, no boots, and no mittens either."

"He's gonna freeze his feet," Ted commented.

"Maybe I ought to put on his boots too," Addy answered. "Pa never did like to wear high top boots. He hated them," Ted said. "I don't think he would take them away from you. And his hands are gonna suffer too."

"We laid the mattress in the middle of the room so maybe he'll walk around that and use his room for walking more. He paces and paces back and forth in there some now."

"Well, that would be warmer anyway," Ted answered.

"What's Linc coming in here looking so mad about, I wonder," Addy said watching him as he came into the room. "You got a problem, or shouldn't I ask?"

"Glad we got the road cleared off anyway. And sure glad we cleared it off south of us. I thought we did it so we could haul hay to the cattle better, but we also made it easier for Clintons and Martins too. Cause they are now using this road."

"Hell, their ranches lay on the other road to town. How come they are using this road?"

"Dan Anderson just told me he heard on the telephone party line that the bridge over the river they cross on their way to Casson went out the other day. Some of the timbers must have been rotten under it and it gave out while Henry Martin was going over it. He didn't get across. The horses did, but the wagon didn't. Dan said Henry got a broken leg out of it. So now they have to use the road past here until spring when the bridge will be fixed."

"If it is then," Ted said, "with money like it is, so tight these years, they might never fix it."

"And you know what," Linc told Addy, "Paul and Marie Clinton came past here just now and they saw me and they didn't wave or nothing. Just looked straight ahead. Never even acknowledged I was there. Made like I was never even standing by the road."

"And when their house burned down, I took them quilts and canning and even took them bread and cookies and baking for as long as it took to get a stove set up for her to cook with in one of the sheds. Well, we can't stop them from using the road, but we can stop making it easy for them. You get those cattle moved down closer to the buildings so you can feed them different. Use the snow plow to plow out a road back to that other pasture. There is that old shed and also that hill with all those trees for the cattle to use for protection. Next time it snows if they want to use this road they can shovel it out up to our driveway."

"Sounds good to me," Linc agreed. "We'll get that done tomorrow morning as soon as Stubby gets the plow back here. Dan gave me another piece of news too. Said he heard Ray Patton has his ranch sold too."

"What's he gonna do then?" Ted asked.

"Move to Casson. Bought a house on the east side of town. One of those big ones, don't know which one, but it's supposed to be really fancy and nice."

"Good riddance," Addy said. "Won't make any difference on the school here or on the feeling with neighbors cause he still owns the mortgages."

"A man from Linksfort is supposed to have bought the ranch. Somebody who lives near there or somewhere around there. Supposed to move in March first."

"Is this where Dan got his news from?" Ted asked.

"Yeah. His brother told him the other day. He heard his grandpa gave him the money on the condition the grandpa would live with them from then on. Dan said Patton wanted to lend him the money to buy the ranch, but the man had the money already and if Patton didn't want to sell it to him, then he'd go somewhere else for the land. And with nobody with money to buy anything, Patton took the offer."

"One less for Patton to have under his thumb," Addy said.

"Right," agreed Linc. "Name of Barlow, the ones buying the ranch."

"Well, you told the Pattons to go and move so I guess one of them is taking your advice, only the move ain't far enough away," Addy laughed as she told Ted.

"You know there have been so many times I've been so glad I didn't marry Ruth. I just shudder to think what she would have done to this ranch, to our family, to Pa, just to everything and most of all what would have happened to me. If I turned out like her old man I think I would have killed myself."

"Unless the change was so slow you didn't know that it had happened," Linc told him.

"Good riddance of all of them," Addy said.

"You're sure as hell right about that," Linc agreed.

One of the hardest things Addy had to contend with now was the physical changes brought about by Martin's refusal to wash himself, shave himself or have his hair cut. His hair was touching his shoulders and his mustache was hanging over his mouth. A brown beard streaked with gray covered his face.

"Sometime I'll have to try and trim that mustache when he sleeps," Ted told Addy softly as he watched her face cringe in dislike as they watched Martin put on his jacket and cap. "And look at his hands. They are bleeding and still he wears no mittens."

"His feet are blistered with chill blanes. It has to hurt to walk."

"That's why he limps now, I suppose," Ted agreed.

"I tried to help him put on his boots, but he won't let me. I even tried them on myself and he didn't seem to care. Course he never did like to wear four-buckle boots. And no mittens either and you can see his hands are bleeding."

"He is walking a lot now in his bedroom, ain't he?" Ted asked.

"Yes, more and more. The door was shut and it took him so long to get it open, and the temper don't seem to be there now like it was. He finally got it open, but he wasn't even riled up, not at all. I thought he'd come a tearing out of there, but he just looked blankly at me, no expression at all on his face. Like he was in a dream."

"Do you suppose we could lock that door and keep him in there some of the time?" Ted asked, "He wouldn't be able to walk outside and maybe his hands would heal and his feet too. We could cut a small part of the door out so heat could get in there. It wouldn't get so cold in there then."

"It would stay fairly warm in there then and if we let him

keep his coat and cap he'd be warm enough, especially for walking around like he does," Addy agreed.

"It would be worth a try," Ted told her.

"Maybe if we locked the door he would walk in there during the day instead of outside in the cold and snow." Addy thought a moment, then added, "It would be worth trying."

"What about meals?" Ted asked. "Do you think he would try to go out then?"

"He don't ever eat with us. I'll just take his food in to him in there. I just hope he don't get his temper back and try to knock the door down."

While mending that afternoon Addy thought about Martin and the locked door. I've got another child, only this is worse. A child will listen to his ma, but a full grown man that don't know nothing is another thing.

"Much worse," she muttered to herself.

Surprisingly, Martin accepted the new arrangement without any problems. Addy always knew when Martin was sleeping because this was the only time footsteps could not be heard in the room.

"I feel like I am feeding a dog," she told Ken and Pete after taking Martin's plate of food in to him.

"But Pa didn't eat with us anyway, for a long time," Ken answered.

"But at least he ate at the table like a man. And I noticed yesterday that he didn't use the fork I gave him and when I looked at his hands, I could see he scooped the potatoes and gravy up in his fingers and ate them that way. I guess I'll have to give him only things he can eat with his fingers now."

"Did he wash his hands?" Ken asked.

"No," Addy answered. "I wiped them off as best I could when he was sleeping."

"Are his hands better now, healing?" Ken asked.

"Yes, they are better. I feel so guilty about all of this, the locking of the door, the feeding in his room," Addy's voice broke as she swallowed tears.

"Aw Ma, you can't help it," Ken consoled her as best he could.

"I know, Ken. And what I feel the worst about is that you will remember him this way and not have all the good feeling about him like Linc and Ted have. And that hurts so much," Addy said, adding, "and that hurts like you wouldn't believe."

Christmas came and went. To Martin it was just another day spent pacing in his bedroom and sleeping on the mattress. For the rest, they did the best they could to make it a nice holiday. Several weeks before the big day, Addy, Stubby and Evie went to Linksfort to shop. This was the first time Addy had been there and she found it a nice experience to have everyone treating her with respect.

Extra sugar was bought for the cookie and candy making. Addy looked for several minutes at the cocoa and finally added a can to her collection of groceries. Then Addy spotted something she had never seen before—a pail marked peanut butter. Picking it up she looked at the label again. She loved peanuts. As a child she could remember her grandpa shucking peanuts for both of them to eat. Noticing another woman stooping to pick up one of the cans, Addy asked.

"Is this good eating? I don't know anything about it. I've never seen it before."

"It's very good on bread if you like peanuts. Kind of greasy—lots of grease on top. You've got to stir it up good to get the heavy peanut mixture on the bottom mixed with the oil on top. My children just love it. I buy it as a special treat."

"Thanks for the telling me. I'm going to take a pail to try."

A gallon of molasses was picked up too and then, thinking how hungry her family would be for the sweet treat, Addy added another gallon.

Longer time was spent in the dry goods store picking out heavy flannel to make work shirts for all the men and also for Ken and Pete. This sewing would be done during those long winter months after the holiday. For Christmas presents she bought a pair of striped overalls for the men and boys, Stubby included.

Time was spent looking at good material, but Addy decided against buying any for Annie or Evie. Not being invited to any of the school doings or any of the neighborhood gatherings put a damper on her decision to buy material for a good dress for each, and everyday dresses and aprons were always made out of feed sacks. Instead she found wool blankets selling for one dollar each. Sorting through the pile she finally picked out two blue ones for Annie and two green ones for Evie. Almost to the checkout counter Addy went back and picked up yarn for a sweater for Annie. Socks were bought for all of the men in her family to replace the worn out patched ones at home.

Realizing she hadn't anything for Sara, she went back and looked at material and at yarn, finally picking out soft pink wool yarn for a sweater. A round teething ring was added to her pile of Christmas presents.

The last items she bought were at the dime store. Several new decks of playing cards for herself and a Chinese Checkers game for the boys. Finding catcher's mitts priced a dollar and nineteen cents apiece, she picked up two that she knew Annie and Linc would be glad to give to Ken and Pete. Searching for something she could buy that Ted could give the boys, she finally found BB air rifles selling for seventy-nine cents each.

Settling down in the car on her way home, Addy was glad she had gone to the can holding her inheritance money and taken out a small amount before she went today. There had to be some joy left in this world, she thought. I can't get any comfort out of living these days, but if I can get a little happiness out of giving a little extra at Christmas, then at least I'll have that much.

Right before Christmas, Ted and Stubby made another trip to Linksfort to get oranges and apples for a special treat. Always a lover of pickled herring, Addy made sure Ted got a small barrel of the raw fish. After cleaning them, she cooked the brine, cooled it and poured it over the fish, along with lots of sliced onions. The spicy sweet-sour aroma of the vinegar solution drifted through the house along with the smell of freshly baked bread, buns, and prune and apple coffeecakes. Deviled eggs were added to the Christmas Eve menu along with mashed potatoes and canned corn she would cream.

After chores Christmas Eve morning, Linc, Ted and the two boys had ridden horses along the river bottoms until they found trees suitable for cutting and decorating. That same morning they were put in stands. Afternoon each household decorated. Evie turned down a tree, but did enter into the festivities by baking all the sugar and molasses cookies and making all the candy. As this was something Evie dearly enjoyed doing, Addy had gladly given her the sugar and other groceries necessary. In her present frame of mind, just making the popcorn balls for the Christmas season's crunching was hard to do.

Chores over on Christmas Eve, the three families enjoyed their supper together at the big house. Martin's meal, as usual, was taken to his room and left, along with the new overalls and socks Addy had bought for him. Whether he would ever wear them remained to be seen.

The rest shared the evening with gift opening, cookies, candy, coffee laced with brandy and hot cocoa. As Evie and Stubby put on their coats, ready to leave, Ted told Stubby, "Sure glad for that snowplow you made, Stubby. Now you can drive home real easy without worry of getting stuck."

"You bet. As long as the ground stays frozen we're all right. Glad I could be of service to you people. I know we had a much better Christmas here than we would have had where we were, but Evie and I had no choice but to live there and this here is real nice. Being with you people, I mean," Stubby replied.

"We are grateful for both of you," Addy answered, walking with them out onto the porch.

"And thank you again for the overalls," Stubby told her.

"Glad you liked them and we all liked the fudge and

divinity, Evie, and the cookies. I am so glad you like to make them. I don't know how much I would have gotten done if I had to do the baking and candy making. If it hadn't been for Ken and Pete I don't know if there would have been any popcorn balls done at all. I just can't muster up much get up and go for that kind of thing this year," Addy told them.

"I enjoyed doing it," Evie said. "And thanks so much for the blankets, Addy, and we will be back for dinner tomorrow."

"Ma, we're going too," Annie told her ma, giving her a big squeeze. "I got to feed the baby yet and I would rather do it at home so I can lay her down without disturbing her much. Merry Christmas, Ma."

"And Merry Christmas to you two, both of you, well, guess all three of you," Addy told them as they went down the steps.

"Ken, you and Pete had better call it a day too. I stuck the soapstones in the oven before, so I'll just get them out and wrap them in the newspapers so you can take them upstairs for your feet," Addy said as she hurried into the kitchen.

"Won't take long to crawl in bed with it so cold up there," Ken told Addy as he took the wrapped soapstone in his hands. "This feels so good, sure feels good on the feet in that cold bed.

"Here Pete, here's one for your bed too. You know if you two slept together you sure would be warmer."

"Who wants to sleep with your brother?" Ken said, his face screwed up in dislike. "This way we each have our own bed."

"Then I guess you'll have to be cold until you warm up the bed yourself. Night. Sleep fast cause there won't be any Stubby tomorrow morning to help with chores," Addy said watching them go quickly up the stairs carrying the kerosene lamp in one hand and the soapstones in the other.

Shutting the door behind them, Addy took two clean

cups out of the cupboard and filled them with hot cocoa. Giving one to Ted, she sat down at the kitchen table and slowly began to sip the hot sweet chocolate treat.

"I was thinking today about when Pa began to act funny," Ted said. "I can't really remember when it was."

"I can't really either. Not an exact time. He was all right yet last year at Christmas. Enjoyed the evening and Christmas Day so much. We even went to Midnight Mass. The weather was good and the roads were just fine. We went then and the rest of you went the next morning while I got dinner. Before lambing time, I felt there was a difference in Martin. He seemed funny already at Easter, although I guess I just didn't notice it so much cause it didn't amount to very much. And then I didn't want to know anything was different anyway," Addy slowly added, "shrugged it off, I guess."

"But he started to walk when the weather got real warm. Dry on the ground. I know I sure thought it odd when he walked that first time, but he said he just felt like it. Didn't want to ride, just felt like walking. I remember how he said it, as plain as if he said it today," Ted remarked.

"And that is when he began to have trouble remembering names. He lost the keys to the car, remember?" Ted nodded his head. "Finally found them in his dresser drawer under everyday hankies. Now why would I put them there, he wondered. He came in onc day and I was cooking sauerkraut. You can smell that all over the house and even on the porch and he couldn't remember what it was. Or how it tasted. I don't know if it had any connection to how he is now, but I remember reading was getting to be a problem last winter. He could read, but he said he didn't know what it said. And his memory used to be so good." After a few moments, Addy added, "Yes, I would say it began a year ago now, give or take a month in either direction."

"So if it has gone this far in one year, then how far will it go by now next year?" Ted asked.

"I don't know. I hate to think about it. Worse! I suppose

like Stubby and Evie's ma. He seemed to accept the change of his walking in his room instead of outside all right and don't seem to mind the door being locked all the time. I feel like I am taking care of a dog. Ken tried to console me one day when I said this and it was so grown up of him to do that. I cried about that when he wasn't around. I didn't want to cry in front of him cause I thought it would make him feel funny."

"You do what you have to do, Addy. It was the only way to make sure Pa stays put in his room at night and didn't beat up anyone like he did the boys this summer. And now it's just a way of keeping him from freezing his feet and hands."

"And Ted, if he got outside at night he would freeze to death," Addy said.

"Yes, he would," Ted agreed. "You want me to try to cut his mustache some while he is sleeping?"

"Do you think you could get some off? At least so it don't hang in his mouth. And maybe some of his hair too. His fingernails and toenails are so bad too. Both of them are so hard that I don't know if they could be cut without soaking some to soften, especially the toenails. Last time they were cut was months ago. And his haircut was for his birthday in March. Cause I said he had to get it cut so he would look nice for his birthday."

"Get a scissor," Ted said. "Let's give it a try." Addy went quickly and got the scissor she used for cutting hair. As luck would have it, Martin was laying on his stomach! Laying a towel carefully around his neck, Ted began to cut the hair on the left side of his head, shaping it as best he could. He then trimmed the mustache carefully and also trimmed the beard on that side. When he had did as much he felt he could, Ted carefully turned his pa's head so he could do the other side. Martin groaned a little in his sleep, but did not show any signs of waking up. Carefully, but quickly he trimmed the hair, mustache and beard on this side of the head. Finally deciding he could do no better, he carefully took the towel away from Martin's neck and they quietly went out the door, locking it behind them.

"We did it. We did it. A hair cut for Martin for Christmas. And I don't think he will even notice or care," Addy told Ted, elated that this had been accomplished.

"How long since it's been washed?" Ted asked.

"Months. But that we'll never get done."

"Go to bed now, Addy. Pa is locked in and sleeping. Tomorrow is Christmas Day and I could care less. And I suppose you even care less than I do."

"Got to have some kind of a day for Ken and Pete. That is why I got a little extra at Linksfort a couple of weeks ago. Just to make the day something nice for them cause they need some kind of memories for the future. We all got to keep going. Got no choice in the matter," Addy replied.

Ted leaned forward, kissing her gently on the cheek. "That's for being the woman you are. I couldn't have wished for a better Ma than Pa got us when he married you."

With tears swimming in her eyes, she chokingly thanked him. Going to sleep she realized she had not returned the compliment. She hadn't told him that she and Annie had found the best family in the world to spend the rest of their days with. Whatever Martin was now, he had been the best husband and lover she could have asked for, before he got sick, before now.

The next day, Christmas Day, the three families spent the day together again. By noon the kitchen at the big house smelled of roasted chicken and bread dressing filled with apple slices and prunes. Addy added baked squash, baked potatoes and gravy to the menu, with squash pie finishing off the meal.

"I know what I want for supper," Ken told everyone when they were finishing eating.

"Peanut butter and bread," Addy answered. "I thought the molasses would be the really big treat and one of the best things I brought home from shopping that day I got all those groceries, but peanut butter is better than that, at least the boys think so."

"I like it too," Linc said.

"You know how he likes it," Annie told the rest. "Most people just are glad to have one thing on their bread, but my husband likes peanut butter for the first layer and then some jelly over that. YUK!"

"Now we know what to have for supper, Addy," Evie told her. "Just put on the peanut butter and jelly and you've got it done."

"I think I'll add the leftovers from dinner too, just for those that like a little more," Addy said laughing. "Although I do have to admit, I once in a while take a teaspoon and have a little peanut butter myself."

"Without bread?" Ted asked, "Nobody eats anything like that alone, you've got to have bread with it. How many times we've been told that, boys?"

"All right. No one heard me say that. I'll have to take bread with it from now on," Addy said, laughingly adding, "I have been put in my place."

The checker boards were put to use by Pete and Ken while the adults played "five hundred" with the new playing cards Addy had gotten. Before the afternoon was over, Ken and Pete were introduced to the game, being taught the fundamentals. Addy was glad they wanted to learn how to play. Before Martin had gotten sick, they had spent many evenings playing "rummy". She missed this pastime. Seeing how the boys were senjoying the card games, she knew she would teach them more card games to help the long winter nights pass more quickly. Although there was always mending to do and sewing waiting for her, Addy enjoyed the challenge of an occasional card game.

Chapter IV

"January now," Stubby commented on New Years Day. "I suppose the rest of the winter is fixing machinery and harnesses."

"Not right away," Ted answered. "Here, sit down. I'll get a cup of coffee."

"Got my boots on and they're full of snow," Stubby answered.

"I'll pull a rug over and then you can sit down," Ted replied. "And then I'll get you that cup of coffee. The first thing we do in January," he said, going to the stove and filling up a cup with the hot steaming liquid, "is to butcher."

"Evie and I wondered when that was done."

"Now. Cold or not, we get it done and then it's over with."

"How many you do at one time?"

"Addy, Linc and I talked about it a couple of days ago and came up with about four hogs, one for you'se, one for Link's and two for the house here. And one beef and that old cow that don't milk much in the barn. We will trim that one out and grind it all. Some is used for raw meat sausage and some for hamburger. Wish we had some way of keeping that raw meat sausage for summer cause that is some of the best eating there is."

Both watched as Addy came out of Martin's room, closing the door behind her. Her expression of depressed hopelessness brought concern of both men.

"Pa worse this morning?" Ted asked, looking toward the outside door as Linc came into the room.

"You got coffee there, Stubby?" Linc asked.

"Sure. Good too," was the answer.

"Get another rug, Addy. I'd take a cup too."

"I'll get the coffee, Addy, and one for you too," Ted told her getting up from the table.

"How is everything at your house?" Addy asked Linc.

"Good. Baby is smiling real nice. Sometimes I can't make up my mind if she is smiling or just gas or just her mouth open. Such a difference she makes at our house."

"In answer to your question before, Ted," Addy said, "Martin seems the same. Boys out doing some chores?"

"They are bedding pens this morning. And can you believe it? One of the cats had kittens a while ago and brought them out now where they can be seen, so they are playing with them when they can catch them. Wild! I don't know how they kept alive in this cold weather. She must have had them where it was warm enough. Usually fall and winter kittens die."

"Most times," Stubby agreed. "Ted and I was talking about butchering."

"Oh yes, that fun job. But I do like meat so that is how it is. We'll get at it Monday. The hogs first and then the beef in the afternoon."

"You mentioned sausage, raw meat I think?" Stubby asked.

"Yes, we make that," Addy answered. "And we make liver sausage. No blood sausage cause nobody likes it. Smoke the hams and bacons and pork chops too."

"Oh, pork chops. That should be good," Stubby commented.

"And make fry down meat out of the pork shoulders. And also make hamburger patties or meatballs and bake them some and then can them. And lard, of course. I think the week we do the meat, Evie will have to help us and forget teaching the boys then. I don't think they will mind and we sure could use her help."

"I am sure she will think that is fine. Do you make tripe?" Stubby asked.

"You boys get the bedding done?" Ted asked as they came into the room.

"And even bedded the pigs with a couple of piles of straw. They started to eat it right away."

"Sounds just like what they would do," Linc answered.

"Did we hear that Evie wouldn't be teaching us when butchering is done?" Ken asked.

"You heard right. But when you have to help with the butchering maybe you'll think it is more fun going to school," was Addy's answer. "You asked about tripe, Stubby? We don't make it as none of us like it. Martin didn't and I didn't and neither did Ted or Link. Ken and Pete never tasted it. We always gave the cow stomach away to Clintons. Paul and Marie love it. They made tripe from our cow stomach and from their own. No way in hell that I will give any to them now."

"If you don't mind, Evie and I really like it. And she would be glad to clean it too."

"She can have the job," Addy told him. "If she and you want the cow stomach then you sure can have it."

"What is tripe, Ma?" Ken asked.

"It's made out of one of the cow stomachs. The stomach is emptied out, washed and washed to get it clean. Then you dunk it in boiling water just right so when you take a fingernail to it, you can peel out the lining or whatever you call it. Evie will take a hog scrapper, like you use to scrap the hair off the pigs. She'll take that and scrap all the stuff off the stomach and when she is done it will be real white and clean. Then she'll cut it up in pieces and cook it until it is done. Then slice it up like noodles and make a sweet-sour dressing for it."

"Evie will can most of it and we'll enjoy it for a long time. Just have bread with it. I can hardly wait to have some. Been a long time since I've had that."

"And sometime, maybe not right away, but before spring and it is still cold outside, we'll cull out some of the old hens and butcher them and can them too. You can tell Evie what our plans are for next week. She can plan to help us."

"And we have harnesses to fix and I know there is some welding to do on some of the machinery too before spring comes," Linc said. "New Years Day. Another holiday today. Sure don't seem like it though. Everyone going to take a nap this afternoon just to celebrate the coming of another year?"

"Not me," Pete said. "Ken and I are going to try to ski this afternoon. Stubby fixed up those two old pairs for us for Christmas and so we're going to try them out."

"We figured it would be steep enough by the bridge and the ice is froze so we would just run into the river."

"I think I'll go with you," Ted told them. "I have a pair of skis up in the attic that are still good, I think. If I can find them, I think I'll go with you. Addy, what you gonna do?"

"Cut out shirts and pajamas so I can start to sew on them yet this week. I think Annie plans on coming up here for supper tonight, don't she?" she asked Linc and he nodded his head yes. "When I mentioned this to Evie she said you and her were just going to stay home where it was warm and not come back," she said to Stubby.

"When I'm done here this morning, I'm going home and that is where we are staying. Not going out at all. Got a little work of my own to do in the barn and in the chicken coop at home."

"Guess coffee time is over everyone," Linc said getting up and putting on his everyday jacket. "Let's get it done."

The following week was full of butchering. By Monday evening the four pigs, a cow and the steer were hanging in the shed cooling. Tuesday gave a breathing spot. Nothing was done on Tuesday except for the noon meal that was fried liver and onions. Wednesday morning Addy cooked the tongue and heart, pickled and canned them. By noon the men were cutting up the pork halves, one by one. Strong salty brine was prepared in the large crocks and the bacons, hams and chunks of pork chops were placed in them, then weighted down with wooden covers to be left for a month or so until the salt seeped through the meat.

Lard was ground and Addy was kept busy cooking. Having never watched this before, Ken and Pete were full of questions and comments.

"Why does the salt make the meat keep? Why are you so careful cooking the lard? Is that where the pork chops come from? Pickled pigs feet? I don't like them. But I sure like fry down meat. Ain't it awful hard to cut those pork halves that are frozen like that? Ain't it cold on the hands?" and "We have to clean up the hog heads? Pete and me?"

"Pete and I," Evie corrected him. "And watch the ain'ts. Use isn't instead. You sound like I am not teaching you anything."

"Cleaning hog heads seems like a good job for you both," Stubby told the boys. "Keep you out of trouble."

"But look at those teeth and what is that? Brains? What we do with them?"

Linc answered, looking around the table at the dancing eyes and laughter in the faces of the rest. "Not all fun and games, boys. Just a lot of hard work including hog heads."

Although all the hogs had been cut up by late afternoon, it would take another day before all the pork had been processed. Pickled pigs feet had to be made and canned the next day. Pork shoulders would be sliced and made into fry down meat to be packed into crocks with hot lard poured over to preserve them until the hot summer days. And all the intestines had to be washed and scraped clean as these would be used for the liver and raw meat sausage casings.

Friday morning was spent cutting the meat off the bones of the cow that had been butchered for trimming. Some was cut into small pieces and canned for stew meat. And some was ground for hamburger and meatballs and the rest would be ground, then well seasoned and packed into casing for the raw meat sausage.

"You don't have to get every little bit of meat off those bones, Evie. We'll cook them up and can the broth for soup. The neck bones are just too hard and take too long, besides they make good soup." Addy told the woman as she watched her.

"Sounds good to me," Evie replied. "I don't like trimming that well anyway."

"What you make out of the steers?" Stubby asked.

"Roasts, steaks and more stew meat for canning," Addy answered.

"Lots of hands sawing," Stubby commented, "and lots of grinding by hand."

"Lots and lots. But good eating," Ted added.

By Friday evening all the meat had been cut. Some of the roasts, steaks and hamburger had been stored in a cold room upstairs where they would freeze. This would provide the meat for the rest of the winter months. A copper bottomed boiler filled with jars of stew meat was cooking on the stove. It would take another full day before all of the stew meat and meatballs were canned.

"And when is the liver sausage made?" Stubby asked.

"Monday," Linc answered. "It will take most of Saturday before all the canning is done and even if we don't go to church anymore, we still won't do it until Monday. Addy will be washing Tuesday this week. Got to use her wash tubs for all the sausage mixing."

"Only Annie washes everyday," Stubby said.

"Yes. Only Annie who has a baby to wash for everyday. Sure is a lot of washing. So many wet clothes from them wetting all the time. And it looks like we'll have another one next year to add to this one. Annie ain't said nothing to her ma yet cause she don't know for sure."

"I won't say anything," Stubby assured him.

"We've got the raw meat sausage to do tomorrow too," Linc told him.

"And when do we get to taste that?"

"As soon as it comes out of the smoke house," Linc answered. "Usually for lunch before we go to bed."

"Sounds good," Stubby answered.

"Annie is going to make crackling cookies tomorrow and some cornbread with crackling in it for breakfast. I can hardly wait. Been hungry for that corn bread ever since Addy started to render the lard."

The rest of the winter months were spent fixing and repairing for the men and for the women sewing, quilting, rug making, knitting and embroidering when there were spare moments. Bleached feed sacks were used to make sheets for the beds, pillow cases, towels for dishes and hands. Some even were made into undergarments such as panties for the women and underwear shorts for the men. Addy crocheted several rag rugs for the bedrooms and started to cut strips out of the men's wool pants for a large braided rug for the front room. This she knew would take several winters to finish if it was going to be as large as she wanted.

In March the days were warmer, starting to thaw the ground. Warm rains toward the end of the month turned the prairie into mud. For several weeks they did not get to town and the ranches were isolated. The gumbo made traveling impossible for any cars or trucks.

"Hope this dries out some before lambing starts," Ted told Addy at breakfast one morning early in April. "There is something I miss so much, and I know I shouldn't say it cause it only makes you feel bad, but I sure miss not having Pa to visit with at meals."

"I know," was her soft answer. "I know. I miss not being able to talk with him at the end of a day right before going to sleep. So many times we went over what happened that day or what was going to happen the next day. I know what you mean."

"I shouldn't say anything like this cause it only makes you feel bad."

"No, I'm glad you do cause then I know I'm not alone in feeling like this. How soon will lambing start?"

"Couple of weeks."

"Weather should be better by then."

And it was. Soon there were lots of bleating lambs running behind their mothers while the herds of cattle were full of white faced calves. Addy's setting hens started to show off their offspring. Flocks of little balls of yellow chicks could be seen cluttering around the old hens. Although she would have enjoyed raising ducks and geese, Addy had long ago given that up. They lived too close to the river that was full of turtles. Even the hogs, not to be outdone, had given birth to baby piglets.

Several days were spent shearing sheep. One by one, Linc and Ted sat the animals on their rumps, leaning them against their legs. Taking a hand clipper they soon had the wool coming off in a single fleece.

"If it wasn't for Dan Anderson's sister Molly we'd be just as far ahead to take this wool and burn it," Linc told Ted.

"Guess she don't mind cleaning it and carding it. Takes a share for her work and then she gets some wool too. Dan said she likes to knit and ain't got money to buy any wool so this gives her some. And we get it done cause Addy don't have the time or the want to take care of the wool."

"What did you used to do with it?" Stubby asked.

"We used to sell it. Packed it into large gunny sacks and hauled it into Casson," Ted answered, stretching while he helped an ewe onto her feet before getting another one.

"This is the first year we took any wool to Dan's sister. But he told Linc she would be glad for the wool. The women will have yarn to knit with and otherwise we'd have to haul it over to Linksfort," Ted answered.

"I think Annie thought my socks would be better mended with yarn than with store string," Linc added. "Store string can be lumpy where yarn is always soft."

"Glad it is drier when we had to start this. Harder to handle the sheep when they are full of mud," Ted said.

"Something I never did," Stubby commented. "Never

sheared a sheep."

"You never did?" Linc asked surprised.

"Nope, always worked with cattle. Never a sheep man. Good thing to get this done cause it looks like we'll be working outside in a couple of days with this warm weather drying everything off so good. Busy working up ground for a few acres of corn."

But no one anticipated the new problems the warm dry weather would bring. Martin was ready to walk again. Addy had opened the bedroom door once the ground had dried out and soon found herself with more troubles. Last year Martin had a purpose when he walked. He had his hiding place along the river to go to. This year he did not remember his hide-a-way, nor anything about the ranch, including how to find his way home. He only wandered, miles and miles. One evening, with everyone searching, he was found near Clinton's boundary fence. Utterly exhausted, he sat on the ground, refusing to move.

"Get the car, Link. Go home and get it and haul him back that way," Addy said. "I'll stay with him."

Late that evening, after Martin had gone to sleep Addy sat at the kitchen table slowly sipping a cup of coffee.

"Can't sleep, Addy?" Linc asked as he came in the door.

"No. Ted ain't home yet. You know the new neighbors, Barlows?" Linc nodded his head yes. "They asked him to come over and help with a horse that was having trouble delivering. He was surprised when they came, but evidently they had been told by Anderson to get us if they needed help. Anyway, he ain't home yet and it's almost ten o'clock. How come you're here and not sleeping?"

"I saw your light. What the hell we gonna do about Pa? We can't spend every night looking for him like we did tonight?"

"I been thinking about that. Either we lock him in his room or we're gonna have to watch him. Linc, I'm tired, dead tired of it all."

"Did you notice how scared he seemed to be of the

horses?"

"Yes. Oh yes, he's afraid of them. And of the cows and anything big like that. Not the sheep. He went right through a flock of them. There ain't no sheep bucks running out there now. Or else that would be a problem too."

"Take turns watching him?"

"I don't know how else to do it. He can't be alone now or he might get in the river and drown."

"Well, Evie won't do it."

"No, she said that when she came that she ain't no nurse and don't want to be and won't be. And that's all right. She offered to help otherwise, like cooking and so that is where she will come in. I think we got to work out some kind of a schedule right now for that. I think I hear the car coming. Must be Ted."

"Yes, it is. Get a piece of paper so we can see what we can work out."

"What is this? Nobody sleeps?" Ted asked coming into the room.

"You look dog tired," Linc said.

"I am. The mare died and so did the colt. Not a very nice night. But one good thing, Addy. They ain't scared of us or Pa. That's stupid, Mrs. Barlow said. Her name is Lillian and his is David. They got one daughter, name of Nellie. She teaches in Linksfort. Anyway, they said after they get settled more, they were coming over. And you had better have the coffee pot on or put it on for them cause they were coming in."

"That will be nice to have friendly neighbors. They realize how the others are?" Linc asked.

"Yes. They had been told all about it by Patton and by others. And they ain't scared of them. They felt sorry for some of the others cause Patton has them scared to death. They said they could see this when they talked to some of them. Money runs everything."

"Well, he ain't chased us out yet. We don't know what else to do Ted, but to work out some kind of schedule for watching Martin. I'll stay with him as much as possible, but I got to have time to eat and wash clothes and clean some too and cook and bake and just keep the house going."

Each person, except Evie, ended up with some time donated each week to keeping an eye on Martin. Even Ken and Pete had their turns. While Martin walked, the rest rode a horse, keeping well back from the man. Last summer he had no trouble finding his way back home in the dark, but this year he was dazed during the day and after dark was utterly lost and confused. As Addy seemed to be the only one that could get him turned toward home, she usually got the late afternoon session.

One day in Linksfort, Ted picked up several whistles. This was another way contact was made between the person watching Martin and the homestead. Ken and Pete had their own way of keeping Martin from wandering too far and soon the others used it to. Whenever the man would wander where he wasn't supposed to be, they would ride their horse near him and he would turn in the other direction. His fear of large animals proved to be an asset.

"You notice, Addy, that Pa is stumbling more and more now. His walking has slowed down so much," Linc told her several months later as they stood watching him leaving the buildings.

"Yeah. He takes so long now to cover what he used to walk in a short time. I've been thinking for some time that I don't think it will be safe for him out here when the bulls are turned out with the cows and the sheep bucks with the ewes even if most of them go up to the other ranches."

"What do we do about it?"

"I wondered if we could put up a fence. Like you put up for a child to keep them from wondering. He always leaves the yard here in one place and if we, or you men, got some more barbed wire and posts, you could fence that in and maybe that would keep him in only one place."

"Good idea. We got money for such a fence, I wonder?"

"I'll find it. Take some out of one of the cans. It would

take some work to put up such a fence, but it could be done and in the long run, look at the time it would save everyone if we knew where he was at all times."

"You notice Pa cries easily now?"

"Yes. And he wet last night too. I had to wash this morning and air out the blanket. I got Ted and Pete to carry the mattress outside so it would dry and air out. I will put something over it tonight to keep it from getting wet again."

"When we go to Linksfort to get the fencing, we'll pick up a rubber sheet. Pa changed his clothes after he wet himself?'

"No. I tried and tried, but I couldn't get him to. It's like the clothes he has on are glued to him."

"He may be confused and dazed, but he's still strong as a bull. I don't think Ted and I could get him to if we held him down."

"It may come to that cause he could get real sore."

"You better know that once that starts, he may wet himself during the day too."

"I can hardly wait," Addy said, sighing.

Chapter V

As Linc had predicted, Martin had gone from wetting himself at night to day time too. After struggling with him night after night, Addy finally got desperate and enlisted the aid of Ted and Linc. They stripped Martin nightly and gave him a bath. Occasionally his hair, beard and mustache were also cut, trimmed and washed. One night they made him sit with his feet in a pan of water and his hands in water until the nails softened enough that they could be rimmed.

Martin seemed to sense when they were going to do something with him and he immediately sat down, wherever he was, outside or inside and would not move. Then when they started to move him, he struggled and fought.

As soon as the five strand fence behind the buildings was finished, they could see it would be a big asset. After Martin walked into the enclosure each morning, the gate was shut and at least they all knew where he was. The time had come to move the bulls onto the range with the brood cows. Soon after that the sheep bucks would be let out amongst the ewes and the knowledge that Martin was penned in and could not get hurt gave a sense of relief to the family.

Addy's only comment after it was finished was, "I suggested it because I knew we had to do something, but I feel like I am penning up a dog. That was the way I felt when I had to start to feed him in his room and this ain't helped that feeling at all."

The security of knowing where Martin was gave Addy some time to spend in the garden. Earlier in the spring she had wondered how she would even be able to have any garden but Evie had assured her she would be willing to put in one for both of them to share. With the men's help the dirt had been plowed and worked up. Ken and Pete had helped plant the potatoes and Stubby had spent many hours helping Evie hoe.

"And when I have the time, what job do I find needs doing first?" Addy asked, looking with distaste at the can she was carrying. "Picking off potato bugs. The job that is the worst."

"The other day, Ken picked them off and I do hope you do a better job," Stubby told her laughing.

"The only good thing about it is that when I get done doing this, then I can take my hoe and pull weeds and work in around the plants. That I will enjoy." And Addy did enjoy the hours she spent pulling the weeds and hoeing around the growing plants. This gave her great satisfaction and soothed her frayed nerves.

The first green onions and radishes had long ago been pulled and enjoyed. The strawberries had ripened. Many meals were just baking powder biscuits with many spoonfuls of the mashed red berries over the top. The rest of the crop were canned in fruit jars to be enjoyed during the long winter season that was coming. Pea and green bean season was over and now they were enjoying sweet corn and the first tomatoes.

Working so close to Evie, Addy reminisced about the good times she had had after she and Martin had married. The neighborhood gatherings, school cleaning picnics,

Christmas programs and end of the school year picnics, were among the things Addy told about. Evie, watching and listening, shrewdly realized Addy was lonesome, not only for Martin's companionship, but also for the companionship of the women of the neighborhood. She knew that her being there eased some of that loneliness, but did not replace the hurt Addy had suffered after the rebuke of friends and neighbors.

One of the days toward supper time when they finished hoeing in the garden, Addy told Evie she wished they could wear overalls and a shirt like the men do.

"You do when you ride," Evie answered.

"I mean all the time. Like working in the garden now. How much easier it would be for crawling around between the rows pulling out weeds if I could wear long pants. My dress and apron are so dirty I'll never get them real clean again. Even with soaking it."

"Well, I suppose you could if you really wanted to, but you'd surely look out of place. Women should look like women, not men," Evie told her warming up to the lecture. "How much respect would a man have for a woman that dressed like he did. A woman's place is in the kitchen and in the home where she wears dresses and aprons. That is a mark of respectability."

"All right, all right," Addy stopped her. "I know I am going to wear the dresses and aprons, but I still think pants and a shirt would be easier. Just look at some of the women that help make hay, work on the wagons and help milk cows and work in the barn like some have to do and in dresses and aprons."

"That's the way it is! That's just the way it is! And we aren't going to change it," Evie answered. "Got enough to worry and think about without trying to change the way men and women are," was her final answer as she started toward the house to wash her hands.

Addy stood a few moments watching her and then chuckling she walked slowly toward the house.

The middle of the summer, the Barlow family came to visit. It had been a bad morning. Having rained for several days before this, Addy had finally locked Martin's bedroom door so he could not get out. Now with clear skies and sunshine, she had opened the door and he was free to venture out again. As if he had lost contact during those days, he did not seem to remember where he always walked. Stumbling down the porch steps, he got to the middle of the yard and turned toward the river.

"Oh no," Addy said to herself watching him. "Not that way, not that way." Something seemed to startle the man and he jerked around, running in a stumbling fashion until he got to the middle of the yard where he suddenly stopped, looked around and sat down in the mud. Knowing she had to watch him, Addy sat down on the porch steps and waited. An hour passed and then another.

"You want us to pick him up and move him to the fence," Linc asked when he came across the yard.

"Maybe that or back into the house."

"Have to completely change his clothes. He's full of mud."

"Plumb full," Addy answered.

"Someone is coming. Riding horses, looks like three people," Linc said, looking down the road.

"Hell and damnation. Just what we need this morning. Can you see who it is?" Addy asked.

"Don't know them at all. Looks like a man and two women," Linc answered.

"Now I wish you and Ted could have moved Martin a long time ago, but I didn't know where you were. I can't believe this. There he sits and we ain't had company for so long and now they are coming in and there he is." Addy's voice cracked with frustration and tears. "Suppose we had better see who it is and what they want."

They watched as the three people rode up. The man was large with dark reddish hair showing beneath his hat. The woman had light blonde hair and seemed much slighter in build. The other woman was much younger with the same dark reddish hair as the man, only slight like the older woman.

Addy and Linc were greeted with three of the friendliest smiles they had seen for quite a while.

"Greetings. We had to come and make your acquaintance," the man said. "I am David Barlow. This here is my misses, Lillian and our daughter, Nellie."

"We are pleased to meet you," Linc answered, shaking the man's hand as he got off his horse.

"We were so glad to get Ted's help the night our mare died. Just appreciated having him come, even if the horse had to die. Nothing none of us could do to save her or the colt."

"Please, come in and I'll make coffee," Addy told them. "And Linc, would you please go down and find Ken or Pete and have them keep an eye on Martin. Please, excuse what you see. I know you've been told my husband is crazy. You've been told about his troubles and as you can see we do have troubles. Nothing we can do about that, anymore than you could save your horse."

"Yes, we've been told," Lillian said. "But we don't care. Bad enough to have all kinds of problems without neighbors making it worse. I was a nurse before I married David and I worked with some of these kind of people so I know what it is all about. There is nothing that can be done when they reach a certain stage. I've seen them sit on the floor just like he is doing. Anyway, we have our hands full at home too. My ma lives with us, has for a long time and she suffers from arthritis, has it real bad. Spends a lot of time in bed, can't walk without help. Has lumps on her hands and feet and her knees are huge. It is so painful. And now David's grandpa is living with us. And he has had a stroke and is in a wheelchair so we have our hands full at home too."

"One of Ma's aunts is visiting us right now so she is taking care of them today. She comes about once a week for a day so Ma can get out and away from it all," Nellie added.

"Yes, then you know how it is too," Addy answered. "When Martin gets like this Ted and Linc just pick him up and move him. This is the first time he ever did this out in the middle of the yard. I didn't know what to do. Here comes Ken and Pete now. They are my sons and they will watch him. Here comes Annie and little Sara. Linc is Martin's son. My daughter married my step-son. And this here is Sara, their daughter. My granddaughter. She's such a good little girl. And as you can see I have another grandchild on the way."

"Pleased to meet you," Lillian told Annie. Holding out her hands to Sara she said, "I suppose I couldn't get you to come to me. I love little babies." Sara timidly let herself be taken by the other woman.

"Good girl." Softly talking to the baby, she followed Addy into the house.

"I put on the coffee pot a little while ago, Addy," Evie told her as the three woman came into the room.

"This here is Evie. She teaches our boys. And her brother Stubby works here, too."

"Glad to meet you. I'd shake your hand, but I've got my hands full of this little one."

"I thought there was a school near here." Nellie said.

"There is, but our boys were asked not to come back to school," Addy answered adding, "well, not asked, told would be a better word for it. Does anyone in the neighborhood know you are here today or that you are speaking to us?"

"Don't make no difference if they do or not," David answered her as the men came in the door. "I told Patton I go where I want. Not where I'm told."

"Well, Patton, the one you bought your ranch from was one of those on the school board that came and told Addy not to send the boys back. Rather, they requested Addy not send the boys back. They would not be responsible if she did. For fighting or whatever. Addy gathered they probably would tell their children to pick fights if they could with Ken and Pete," Linc said.

"Evie is a real good teacher. I know they learned more this past year than if they had gone back to the school. It only makes me mad that our tax dollars support that school and our boys can't go there."

"I agree with you, Addy. Patton tried to warn us too, but since we bought the ranch, had the money for it, he laid off and quit. He wanted to sell real bad and Grandpa had the cash. Said he was going to move to town and then probably get into politics. Maybe run for state senator."

"Politics would be just right for him. That would be something he'd be real good at. He'd fit in real good," Linc answered. "I think Ted is coming. Got another cup for him, Annie?"

"I wondered whose horses those were," Ted said, shaking David's hand. "And you must be Nellie, the teaching daughter."

"Yes, Pa has said again and again how glad he was you came that night."

"Glad to be of help. Everything all right, Addy?"

"If you mean Martin, no. That is where he sat and I can't move him. Annie, please take out a piece of coffeecake for both Ken and Pete. Thanks. They eat like there is no bottom to them. Growing so much."

"I ain't figured out why the neighbors fall in line with Patton so much. I know lots of times that someone will run a neighborhood, but these ranchers seem to be afraid of him," David wondered.

"Cause he has lent them money and threatened to foreclose on them if they don't do what he says," was Ted's answer.

"That figures. Now we know why," David answered, nodding his head yes.

"And the bank in Casson is run by his brother and there is money lent there to different businesses. They got the same message so we had to change towns to do our business in. We go to Linksfort, much farther, but so much nicer," Linc told him.

"How did you find out this ranch was for sale?" Addy

asked.

"Through Lillian's brother-in-law. They own the feed mill in Linksfort and Dan Anderson told him he had heard Patton wanted to move to town," David answered. "We still do most of our business in Linksfort cause that is where we did it before and most of our friends are there too so we just kept on going back there and now I think we will just stay there. Know anything about the bank here, other than it is run by a Patton?"

"No," Ted answered. "We don't do business in town here at all and don't get a newspaper or have a radio so don't get any news. Don't visit with neighbors any more so we are really by ourselves. Kind of like an island, alone."

"Many rumblings about bank closings all over. Hear it all the time. My brother-in-law said he heard rumblings about the Casson bank for some time already."

"Ma," Ken came and softly called to Addy through the screen door," Pa is walking toward the barn."

"You got your things to take care of and we got to go too." David said getting up. "Glad to meet you folks and you just don't forget that we are your neighbors and friends. Come on Nellie, Lillian." With this he shook everyone's hand and they walked out to their horses.

"Breath of fresh air," Addy told Evie as they watched them ride out of the yard.

"Addy," Evie said one day after they had spent hours canning. "I am almost out of soap at home. Is there any here I can buy? I have to get some the next time I go to town or have Stubby bring me some when he goes. Anything I hate, it's trying to wash dishes without soap."

"I've got some left. I've got lots of grease and tallow from butchering last winter and what I've saved for a couple of years to make more. It's a job I just hate so I put if off as long as I can," Addy answered.

"I know you've got the big kettle on the edge of the yard. I'll tell you what. I don't mind doing it. Stubby always helped me before so if I can have his help for a couple of days, then I'll make some."

"I'll check with Ted and Linc and see when they can spare him. I would like it if you would, cause I really hate that job. Just staying by that kettle for hours at a time seems like such a waste of time. Always dinner to get or something else that should be done too, and once it starts to boil you can't move from it for three long hours."

"If Stubby can help me, maybe we can make up all the grease there is. You got lye here?"

"Linc is going to Linksfort in a couple of days. I'll have him get some. Tell you what, first thing tomorrow morning, we'll weight up what old grease we got and you bring your grease too and we'll see what we have to have in lye."

When Evie was collecting her old grease, she found several cans of lye. Weighing out twelve pounds of grease, she added five pints of cold water and the lye and made herself two batches of cold water soap to tide her over until more lye could be bought at the store.

"I never made soap that way," Addy told her.

"It is quick and it is an easy recipe to use when you don't have much to make," Evie answered her. "When you've got lots to make, then the cooking way is a better way to go. Some day when I have more time, lots more time, I'll even make some fancy good smelling soap with perfume in it or whatever else I can find that will make it smell good."

"Now that would be something extra special," Addy answered.

"But for now we'll just cook the rest in the big kettle and get it done."

Evie and Stubby made soap for five days straight until they had all the old grease and tallow used up. First thing in the morning, Stubby carried the water needed to the kettle and then started the fire underneath it. Adding the grease and lye, he and Evie took turns stoking the fire and stirring the mixture. After it came to a boil one of them watched it carefully and when it started to boil hard, they stirred vigorously to make sure it did not boil over. After three hours cooking, the fire was to let go out and the soap sat in the kettle until the following day.

The next morning , Stubby, using a large butcher knife, cut the white soap that had come to the top of the kettle, into long slabs that he could lift out. Putting the long pieces into a box, he carried it up to Addy's attic where he cut it into bars and it was left to dry.

The watery waste that was on the bottom of the kettle was scooped out and thrown over the fence. Then water was put back into the kettle and the whole process was started over again.

Five days later the final batch was cooked and the job was done.

"I am so glad that is finished," Addy told both of them. "I hate that job and you both did it so good. Now we'll have soap for a long time again, even dividing it between the three houses."

"And it does smell so good," Evie said.

"Smells so clean," Addy added. "A nice clean smell."

On their next trip to Linksfort, Ted found out that Ray and Joe Patton had been there.

"Can you imagine, Addy, they went to a lot of the businesses there and tried to get them to blackball us. I was told about it at the feed mill. Patton didn't know that Clark is a brother-in-law of the Barlow's. They also went to the dry goods store, both grocery stores and the hardware store. The only thing the Pattons didn't know was how everyone is related in that town. Seems like most of the store owners are related one way or another, shirt tail."

"I just can't believe they would stoop to that level just to get rid of us," Addy said, her eyes wide with disbelief.

"Clark said the best was when they went to the banker and the mayor. Invited him and the mayor to dinner, lunch I guess you call it if you're in the right class of people. Anyway, banker to banker Joe Patton warned about doing business with us. Cause we got a crazy man living here. Well, the banker looked at the mayor who got real mad. The mayor's wife, just died about two weeks ago, and they had to hire people to watch her all the time cause she was crazy, worse than Pa. She tried to kill everyone all the time, taking sharp knives, trying to cut people and stab them. The mayor just got up and walked out on the meal. Left just like that."

"He didn't tell them off?" Addy asked.

"No. Just told them to forget he ever met them. And then the banker told them about the mayor's wife and I guess they realized then that maybe they had made a mistake. Money sure goes to some people's heads," Ted said. "I bet their main reason for going over there was to get support for Ray's running for state senator. From what I gathered this was going fine until they started to run us down. Then they hit bottom. Mainly because of Barlow and Anderson's relatives and of course the mayor and banker. I didn't realize quite all of this until I stopped at Barlow's on the way home and got invited in for coffee and then we discussed it all very well. Had some real good cookies there too. Nellie made them."

"Now that is a girl worth thinking about. I wouldn't be afraid if you would look there once or even twice."

"Oh I am looking," Ted answered laughing. "And while I was there I asked her if she'd like to go horseback riding Sunday."

"And?"

"And I am meeting her near the river at one o'clock."

"Good for you. Now you're doing something I approve of."

"Thanks," Ted laughed as he went out the door, adding, "thanks, Ma."

"Weather feel funny to you?" Linc asked Stubby one hot muggy afternoon about a month later.

"Yep, sure does. Just not right. Thought that all day. Just right for a storm," was the answer.

"Feels like tornado weather, only wrong time of year. That comes early in the year, like April, May and June. Not now in August."

"There ain't nothing saying they can't come then too,"

was Stubby's answer.

"Don't need it though. Not hail either. Ted tells me you found another sheep dead this morning."

"Yeah. Dog been killing them I would guess. Going to have to keep an eye out for a stray dog," Stubby answered.

"You think only one dog?"

"I think so. Looks like it to me. Would be more killed each time if it were more than one. I found tracks down by the river and there was only one set."

"We'll have to watch." Looking around the sky, Linc added, "I sure am glad we got that hay in yesterday, but with the winter wheat ready to cut and shuck, we don't need some bad wind or hail."

"Or worse," Stubby added.

Later in the day, storm clouds gathered. Keeping an eye on the approaching storm, Martin was brought back into the house long before supper. Doors on buildings were shut and the wash brought in from the line.

Long streaks of lightning could be seen in the distance getting closer and closer. Gusts of wind sent whirlwinds of dirt chasing across the yard. The first bursts of rain brought with it hail, followed by heavy rain. In a few minutes the storm was over.

"Not as bad as we thought it could be," Addy told Ken and Pete. "Glad it wasn't anything else. Looked so funny all day." But the storm had done damage. Both Ted and Linc had watched from the barn as a strip of hail running east of the buildings flattened whatever lay in it's path.

The next morning Linc found damage to the winter wheat crop and extensive damage to some of the hay fields. He also found a large dog, a collie, near one of the flocks of sheep. The dog, not paying any attention to Linc's horse, cautiously worked it's way nearer and nearer to the animals. Getting off his horse, Linc slowly walked closer, keeping well above the dog and the flock. Gun in hand, he kept a steady watch. When he saw the dog crouch and then attack, he shot. His bullet stunned the dog. Quickly shooting again, the dog rolled in death.

Kicking the dog over, Linc shook his head in disbelief. Clinton's prize dog. Damn! He quickly got on his horse and headed home.

"Ted, you busy?"

"Yeah, I was going to fix this here grain binder. Why?"

"Get your horse and I'll get two shovels. We've got to bury a dog."

"You get that killer dog? In the daytime?"

"I sure did and it's Clinton's prize dog. We got to bury that sucker deep, real deep so nothing ever digs it up. If they find out I've shot that dog there will be hell for sure."

By dinner time the two men had buried the dog. Just to be sure nothing disturbed the hole, they checked it for many days to come. They never heard if Clintons missed their dog and they never asked nor told anyone except Stubby what happened.

A week later the weather broke loose again. Seeing dark clouds coming late in the afternoon, they watched a greenish haze gather at the edges. This time Addy could not get Martin to come in, and finally Ted carried the man to the car and hauled him back in the house. Intent on staying outside, Martin knocked Ted over and lumbered back outside again and toward the barn. Ted went after him, picking him up and putting him over his shoulder. Martin pounded him with fists and feet. Getting him into the bedroom, Ted shut the door and locked it. Going back outside, he could see Addy and boys still watching the sky.

"It's so still. Just like all hell will break loose," Addy told him.

"There is plenty of wind in those clouds. They're just churning and if they come down there will be plenty of damage everywhere," Ted answered. "Where are the rest?"

"Annie is coming now with Sara. Linc went to Linksfort and Stubby and Evie went home. He had to check on a cow and said he would be back later," was Addy's reply.

"And here comes the start of the wind," Ted said. "We'd

better get down to the cellar."

"I won't leave Martin," Addy told him.

"I'll get him," Ted answered running into the house. Unlocking the bedroom door, he pushed Martin into the kitchen.

"It's bad out there," Addy said, hurrying to open the trap door that was in the pantry floor.

"I sometimes wondered if we would be better off up here than trapped down there if the house would come down on top of us," Ted said. "Come on, Pa. Annie, go first and you too, Pete. Ken, you go down part way and then take Pa's feet cause I'll have to take him under the arms cause he ain't going to walk down. I can see that."

"I am glad the cellar door is inside the house," Annie said adding, "Ma, where is the lantern before we shut this door?"

"I've got it. Ted, blood on your face?" Addy asked.

"I guess so. Pa scratched me getting him down here. He was kicking and scratching when I carried him in the house and again now. Only now he managed to get at my face. He's got fingernails that are like knives."

"You said you were glad the cellar door was inside the house," Ken said to Annie. "Why? I would have thought it easier to get to the cellar outside the house. Easier to get Pa carried down."

"Cause of rattlesnakes," Annie answered.

"Oh. I never thought of that," Ken replied, awed at the thought.

"I remember the cellar that Frank had, your pa," she told Annie. "That cellar was outside and never fixed up much, so there were places where the snakes could have gotten down into the cellar. I was always afraid to go down there to get potatoes or anything after the weather got warm. I felt in the winter that the snakes went to sleep, but in the summer they were awake and I was afraid. And so I was glad when this trap door was in the pantry. It's nice in the winter too to get potatoes, carrots and canning without having to go outside in the snow."

"But not so nice should the house fall down on us," Pete piped up.

"I don't think that is going to happen today," Ted assured him. "In a few minutes I'm going to stick my head out and see what is going on."

When Ted finally did open the trap door it was to find the wind had died down and it was only raining. The family found the yard a mess. Broken limbs and downed trees lay on the ground. Part of the roof from the hog house had been torn off and lay against the barn. One old elm tree was laying across the top of the chicken coop, completely destroying that building.

"I'll bet we find dead hens in there," Addy said.

"Maybe not cause the hens like to crawl around on the machinery in that other shed. That's where we find most of the eggs too," Ken told his ma.

"I'll just bet we don't have to wonder where to cut firewood this winter. There has to be plenty of trees down along the river." And Ted was right. The tornado had cut a path across the prairie east of the buildings. It continued across the river bottoms, pulling many trees out by the roots. The family was thankful the storm had missed their buildings and the buildings on High Ranch and Big Mile Ranch.

"We'd better check fences tomorrow," Ted told Pete and Ken. "For tonight we'll move stock into the pasture by the barn." They watched Linc walking into the yard.

"Can't get the car any farther. I'm stuck in the mud."

"That don't surprise me. We'll get the team and pull it home," Ted answered. "I was telling Pete and Ken we'd better move the stock down to the barn pasture cause we don't know what damage there is on the fences and I don't want any of our cattle over in the neighbor's pastures."

The next morning Stubby, Ted, Ken and Pete rode out with fencing equipment to check the fences. The farther they went, the more destruction they could see. Pieces of lumber from buildings were strewed along the way. Coming upon the line fence they shared with Clintons, they found Paul Clinton and his son, Mark, fixing the fence.

"Paul, some of this here fence is ours so we'll fix this part. Looks like you've got problems at home."

"Yes," Paul answered. "All the buildings are down and..."

"Be careful, Pa," Mark interrupted. "None of their business. As long as they want to do the fence, let's go home. You be sure and fix it up good, you hear! We don't want to come back and find any of your cattle on our ranch."

"You won't," Ted assured him "You need any help, just let us know. None of our buildings went down."

"We don't need your help, now or any time." Mark sharply answered. Noticing his pa was going to say something, he rudely continued, "As long as Martin is like he is, I, or we, don't want you to set foot on our land, any of our ranch," pointing toward the ground on his side of the fence.

"Ain't that something," Stubby said, as they watched them mount their horses and ride away.

"Foolishness," Ted said adding, "and what the hell did we ever do to them? Ma and Pa always took them things like food when they were sick and were good neighbors to them."

"Pete and me were riding along this fence the other day looking for gophers, Ted. And we saw Ruth, the one you were going to marry. She was with Mark Clinton, riding together. We wondered if it was Ruth and we snuck up behind that clump of wild plum bushes and hid," Ken told Ted.

"We put our horses where they couldn't see them," Pete added, "and it was her all right. We know her from when she came out to our ranch when you were seeing her."

"Well, that explains a lot," Stubby told Ted. "Wonder if her old man and his bank will put up the money to build back that ranch?"

"One happy family," Ted answered. "Just glad it's him with her and not me. And yes, I'm sure her old man will put up the money, him and his bank."

Chapter VI

Plans can be made, worked on and forecast. But sometimes they just don't work out as they were projected. Yes, as Ted and Stubby had predicted, the Casson bank would loan the money to Paul Clinton to rebuild. And Ruth Patton's engagement to Mark Clinton was announced among much fanfare and publicity. Ray Patton officially put his name into the political arena in his bid for state senator. And the State Bank of Casson closed it's doors permanently one afternoon after the State Department of Banking made a visit. Every depositor in the bank would in all probability lose most of what they had deposited. And it was a certainty that the shareholders were out every penny they had invested.

The news hit the Rafferty Ranch the next morning when David Barlow and his brother-in-law, Bob Clark, who owned the feed mill at Linksfort, drove into their yard.

"What brings you here," Addy asked, coming from the house eager to greet the unexpected yet very welcome guests.

"Got some news, Addy. Where are the rest?" David

asked.

"Ted and Stubby took Ken and Pete with them to check cattle on Big Mile Ranch. Linc is doctoring a sore foot on one of the horses by the barn. You want me to get him?" she asked.

"Nope. We'll go down and get him. If it ain't too much trouble, put the coffee pot on and we'll come back."

"I was hoping you'd let me in on the news, or whatever you have to tell."

"We will."

"Company, Ma?" Annie asked, "I saw the car and since we don't have much company I had to come and see who it was."

"David Barlow and Bob Clark, who owns the feed mill in Linksfort. They went to get Linc. Got some news of some sort. They asked me to put on the coffee pot. Get some of those cookies Evie made yesterday. Hi there, little girl," Addy said, putting her finger out to the little girl. "Look at her. Standing by that chair. Won't be long before she's walking. She should walk by the time she's a year old. In two months, sure, she'll be walking by then. Good thing too, with another one coming right after that."

"Here they come back," Annie said.

"Just sit around the table. You must have had the horse done?" Addy asked Linc.

"Just done."

"Annie sit here and I'll get the coffee. Take some coffee and cookies and pass them around. Now David, you've got my curiosity riled up. What's the news? We get so little around here," Addy said.

"Well, Bob is the one who told me," David answered.

"And Dave Lay, my banker, told me. You know him?" They nodded yes. "He had just come back from Casson last night. Came back on the train. Casson's bank closed it's doors yesterday afternoon. The State Department of Banking, I think that's what it is called, come in at noon and closed the doors in the afternoon. It went belly-up. Done! Finished! And," Bob continued, "Joe and Ray Patton got into a fight at Ray's house and Ray took a gun and shot Joe. And then shot himself."

"In one of the bedrooms in Ray's house he just moved into," David added.

"Oh my goodness," Addy said, horrified.

"Are you sure about this?" Linc asked.

"Dead sure cause Dave Lay talked to the constable and that is how it went. Mrs. Ray Patton screamed and screamed until someone put her to bed."

"And Dave told me that everyone who had money deposited in it probably will lose all of that. And the stockholders, I am told, won't get back a cent."

"I asked Dave what happens to the ranchers and those who had notes at the bank and he said they would be called in by a receiver who takes over the bank. If the ones owing the notes can't pay up, then they foreclose on them."

"What do you mean called in?" Annie asked.

"I mean they have to pay up what they owe or else the receiver will foreclose on them."

"Clinton's buildings? He did borrow to replace them," Addy commented.

"He did borrow. Dan Anderson told me that a couple days ago in Linksfort. He got all the money needed to build again from the bank. He had the carpenters starting on the house and barn this coming week. Guess he thought about not building cause he didn't know if he could pay back a loan on a penny-or-so-a-pound cattle, but Patton told to rebuild and take his time about paying it back," Bob told them.

"And now what?" Annie asked.

"Where is he going to get the money to pay that back?" Addy asked.

"If he hasn't started then I suppose he didn't use the money up," Bob answered.

"Pattons must have lost all their money too. And that is why Ray shot his brother and then killed himself. But that don't make any sense," Addy said adding, "Martin said Joe used his share of his pa's money to start the bank. He thought he owned all of it. Ray's money from his pa went into land. He bought his pa's ranch and then Martin said he bought two large ranches north of here in South Dakota. And he had loaned money to ranchers around here, Boyen and Clark, for instance. Why would he want to shoot Joe? He ain't penniless. He has money."

"Lay said Ray had sold those ranches in South Dakota a while ago and used that money for loaning to ranchers around here. What money he didn't loan out to ranchers around here, he put into Joe's bank. Lay knows this for a fact. He knew the banker from up by one of these ranches Ray owned, and he told him Ray had sold the ranch up there. And the other one too."

"All right. He would have lost the money he had left from the sale of the ranches. What wasn't used for loaning out to ranchers around here. But would that be enough to make him shoot Joe?" Linc asked.

"From what Lay said, Ray needed money to finance his political career. He wanted to use some of the money he had under interest at Joe's bank. The two brothers were arguing over this when they had that meal together at Linksfort, when Ray was trying to gather support for his campaign."

"And get us kicked out of Linksfort," Annie added.

"And that too," Bob agreed, "anyway, Joe didn't want Ray to use any money out of the bank that was under interest. Lay said with the bank closing now it makes sense cause Joe needed every cent he could get just to keep the bank stable. Anyway, he must have talked Ray out of taking any money out of there. Instead, the bank took over the mortgages Ray had on the ranches around here and Ray got the money for them. When Ray sold his ranch, most of that went to pay for that fancy house he bought. What little was left he had already used politicing."

"And so he didn't have any outside money coming in from payments on the mortgages cause he had turned them over to Joe's bank in return for the cash. So when the bank went belly-up he lost everything too along with Joe,"

David said.

"I know it ain't very Christian, but I just can't help not feeling bad about those two. They made life so miserable for us, I just can't feel anything but relief that they are gone. And that is sinful to think that way."

"But I can see why, Ma," Annie told her.

"We've got to be on our way home, David. These are good cookies," Bob told Addy.

"Thank you. But you've got to give Evie the credit for that. She made them yesterday. I canned all day. Evie's my salvation. I don't know what I would do without her."

"Martin no better?" David asked.

"No. If anything worse. I won't even think about how much worse it can get. We sort of live that day by day, as it comes. I don't know where it will stop. But Stubby and Evie's ma had the same thing and it got bad, real bad."

After a little more visiting the two men left. The rest sat around the table a while longer just talking and thinking about the news they had just been told.

All of this was rehashed again that evening after Ted and Stubby got back. The next day Ted and Linc made a trip to Andersons to see what they knew and it was the same as they had been told the day before. Dan felt a good many businesses in town and many of the ranches would be bankrupt before it was all finished. Rumors were everywhere.

"One day a millionaire and the next day a pauper," Addy commented, at the supper table that Sunday evening. This was Nellie's first visit as Ted's guest. He had gotten her early in the afternoon to spend the rest of the day with the family. She obviously enjoyed her visit. Addy found her a joy to have around. The comparison between Ruth Patton and Nellie stood out so sharply.

Ruth had put herself out to be nice, but there was always the feeling that she was beneath herself when she came. Nellie's laughter, fun and common sense came shining through. And her acceptance of Martin, for this Addy could have hugged her.

"And when do you go back to Linksfort?" Addy asked.

"Pa will take me back early tomorrow morning so I am there by eight o'clock or so. School starts at nine o'clock and I room about a block from the grade school. I'll put the food that Ma sends with me away and then rush right over to school."

"You like teaching don't you?" Annie asked.

"I do like teaching. Those little ones are so nice. I teach first through fourth grade. Another teacher, Mrs. Powers, teaches fifth through eighth. I have twenty-one students and she has twenty. I think next year there will be more coming in, as it looks like one of the schools way up on the gumbo will be closed. They have only four pupils in the whole school this year and one of those families is moving next spring. If no one else moves in with a family, that school will close and those children will have to board somewhere in Linksfort."

"That many children must make for a very full day, with grading papers and doing lessons," Addy commented.

"It does, but what else do I have to do with my evening? Mrs. Powers is a widow and her children don't live around here so her evenings are pretty empty too. She said she didn't know what she would do without teaching because she'd have nothing to do with her time."

"What does she do in the summer?" Ted asked.

"Visits her children, a while here and somewhere else for a while. She has five, I think."

"That would be different, wouldn't it?"

"Yes, it would. I come home when the roads and weather let me and sometimes it can be weeks before I get home in the winter. The time is long, especially Saturday and Sunday. Then I knit, crochet or sew to fill my time. And I hate to leave now, but I think I had better go home, Ted. Ma wants to get everything ready tonight for me to take back."

"I'm so glad you could come today," Addy told her. "And I'm so very thankful that you understand about Ted's pa."

"You haven't seen my grandpa, Pa's pa. Ma has her hands full with him. But he bought them that ranch so Ma will give him very good care. She does such a good job with Grandma. I stayed there yesterday so Pa and Ma could go shopping. It's hard for Ma to get away, even to get groceries. And like you people, they don't go into Casson, so it takes a lot longer to get to Linksfort."

"You come again," Addy told her giving her a hug.

"I will," she said quickly looking at Ted. His smile and the nod of his head yes assured Nellie and all the family that she would be back.

The next time Linc saw Dan Anderson he came home with the news that the Clinton ranch was coming up for sale. The money they had borrowed for the buildings was only part of the money that was owed the bank. A sheriff's auction would be held on the courthouse steps, probably by the end of October.

"How much will it go for, you suppose?" Addy asked Ted.

"Don't know. Maybe around twenty-five hundred to three thousand dollars. I'm only taking a guess. There ain't hardly any buildings left so it may go for less. Course I don't know who will buy it cause there ain't no loose money anywhere for people to use for buying ranches. Heard tell Henry Martin would like to buy it, but he ain't got any money either. His missus is against it, but she never did have anything to say. If she'd had anything to say, that kid of their's would have been made to mind, but guess she had to learn a long time ago to keep her mouth shut. Henry thinks the kid will stay home and work if he could buy the Clinton ranch, but he don't work at home or anywhere, I guess. Does nothing, but go and raise hell."

"I was just wondering. I got inheritance money left," Addy told him.

"Sure you want to use that for more land?" Ted asked smiling.

"I kind of hate to use more of it too. It's nice for an emergency. But it would be nice to get more land and the neighbors farther and farther away. Henry Martin, he's worse than the Patton's, only he ain't got any money. If that is what it would go for, then we could buy it. And have money left over."

"Annie said the other day that the figures look all right on the books. At least we ain't going in the hole, but I know cattle ain't worth anything much," Ted answered.

"Count the cattle that are left to sell. We've sold to the butcher shop so I know some are gone. And let's see how much we got. What we can come up with for money. Sheep ain't worth anything. We give them away. But we've got extra horses for sale this fall again. We've got a reputation for good horses, got to sell farther away than around here. At least at Linksfort maybe we could sell them."

"I won't want to get down to our last dollar. Not have a little on hand when we need it, Addy. I don't ever want to eat words like I told Patton, even if he ain't here to hear them."

"I know that, Ted. I don't want to either, but if we can get that land, I would be glad."

By counting everything, by figuring down to the last penny, by selling cattle at the sale barn, some horses to several doctors and several ranchers, and with Addy's inheritance, the Rafferty's were able to come up with what they felt would be sufficient money to buy the Clinton Ranch and have money left over.

But when Ted spoke to Dave Lay, the banker at Linksfort, he proposed several things.

"Some of the businesses in Casson are going to be sold at the sheriff's sale too. Included in these are the feed mill and the creamery. I believe the hardware store is going too. I have others that would be interested in putting some capital into a corporation and buying these buildings. I wondered if you folks would be interested. And there is also the Boyen and Clark Ranch going up for auction."

"That is going to be sold too?" Ted asked.

"Oh yes! Also Daffy's. Doesn't his ranch lay next to High Ranch?"

"Yes, it does. Can you make a visit out to our ranch and talk to all of us? We need to think about this further and also see how much money would be needed to put into the corporation. This is information we all need."

"It would be faster and easier if you and your brother came here," he was told.

"There ain't anything we would do without Addy's knowing about it and having her say about it. You see, Mr. Lay, we have a different situation than a lot of ranchers do. Our step-mother is a very important part of our ranch and decisions. And so is Annie, Linc's wife. For one thing, Addy's money bought both of the ranches we have on the gumbo. And she still has inheritance money left and it was her that wanted to buy Clinton's ranch. I was sent to put out feelers and to see what information I could find. I know at most houses the women have nothing to say about anything, but Linc and I don't do that at ours. You would see smoke way over here if we tried that. And because Pa's sisters were so nasty when their pa died, and one said that she would get our ranch back after our pa died, our pa sold the ranch, the home place, to Addy for one dollar, and the machinery for another dollar with the provision that Addy would take care of him and he would live there until he died. He did that a few years ago before he got sick and that is the only thing that saved our ranch when Pa got sick."

"There is a will leaving everything to you and Linc when she dies?" Dave asked.

"To all four sons. We have two brothers that are younger, our half-brothers. And Annie, Linc's wife, is Addy's daughter. But she gets some inheritance from another relative when they die. That has been made out a long time ago. Addy's people had money and she has used it to make our ranches bigger and better. There is no way that we would even think of leaving her out of any decision making. And Annie, in case you didn't know it, does all the book work."

"Unusual," Mr. Lay commented.

"But very good. More heads make better decisions."

"Yes, as long as they can agree. I could tell you many stories. I'll be over Monday morning."

"I'll tell Addy to keep the coffeepot hot," Ted told him as

he shook his hand before leaving the bank.

The following Monday morning, the family gathered around the kitchen table. Evie and Stubby, not wanting to be around when the meeting was held, took off for Linksfort to do shopping and visiting. Ken and Pete had the morning off from their school studies so they were out riding.

"I know you are thinking of buying the Clinton ranch, Mrs. Rafferty, but I want you to think about something else before you decide for sure," Dave Lay told the group. "There are buildings, rather businesses, in Casson that are going to be sold at the sheriff's sale along with ranches. Among them are the feed mill, the creamery, and also the hardware store. I think these can be all bought for practically nothing. I know of no one in Casson that has the money to buy any of them. I don't know of any one person in Linksfort that has the money either. They maybe would like to own them, but they don't have the money to even think about it. Since Ted was in the other day, I nosed around Casson a little, well, quite a little," he added smiling, "and got all this information. The bakery is going to be all right because they don't owe money to anyone. And the grocery store is all right too, as far as I can see. The shoe store is in good shape, as good as any these days. And you know the men's hat store and the women's millinery stores are already closed. Larson's dry good store now carries men's and women's hats. The hardware store is going up for auction. Tom Raymer, who owns the Allis Chalmers dealership and is also mayor, is in excellent shape considering the hard times we are in now. The creamery and the feed mill would be the best ones to buy. Before you even think about putting money into this corporation, I think you've got more than enough money to buy both the Clinton, and the Boyen and Clark ranches with money left over. There are three people thinking that they are going to put money into a corporation with the purpose of buying these businesses. We need another, or would like to have a fourth party in this corporation. We would like you, the Rafferty's to be the fourth party.

"Both the Clinton and Boyen-Clark ranches are going up for sale?" Addy asked.

"Yes. I hate to tell you that because we had hoped to pick up our fourth partner here, but yes, I do think so."

"How much do you think those buildings would go for and what about the contents of the buildings? The screws, bolts, nails, hammers and whatever is in a hardware store. And the feed mill, that has the flour grinding mill in it besides being set up to grind feed for cattle. They sell salt, cotton cake and things like that. And the creamery has the ice cream equipment besides butter making and they bottle milk for sale. How does all that work?" Addy asked.

"I would guess the creamery would go for three thousand at best. The hardware store, maybe a thousand or less cause the building is old. There is a fair amount of inventory in there. That would be worth probably five hundred dollars. And the feed mill, again I think three thousand would buy it. Added together that makes seven thousand. A lot of money. Yes, a lot of money."

"I don't think buying any of those businesses would make it easier to go back to Casson. I still think there are too many bad feelings there. The poison is still there," Addy told him.

"Oh, I think you are right about that. But we wanted to make sure we knew who was taking over these businesses. Make sure no Pattons or Patton followers get them. And then when other businesses come up for sale, and they do with people dying or moving, then we would be ready to step in again."

"How much money is each party putting in?" Linc asked.

"Two thousand each. That makes eight thousand. I know that is a lot of money, but it will take some to buy those businesses, and a little, probably a hundred or so to pay wages and keep inventory during the first month after the transition. The rest would stay in a savings account and be ready for the next time needed. After I tell you who the people involved are, I think you will know they and I are honest people only interested in cleaning up the town of

Casson."

"Who manages this sale?" Annie asked.

"How is the sale completed and who does the buying? Cause we can't do it, not with the buildings nor with the land, as I told you the other day," Ted asked.

"Tayor. He is not involved in the corporation, but he will be the lawyer for it. And I would think he would be the one to buy the land for you. The corporation will be managed by me. I will be the president at least for now. In a few months we will have an election of officers. Each month you will get an asset and liability sheet. Assets are what you own and liability is what you owe. These would be monthly with a meeting of the corporation quarterly, every three months. It can be in Linksfort or it can be here. Probably would be better here cause then no one would wonder why we are all getting together. The corporation will buy the buildings or businesses. No other names will be given. If anyone is curious to know who the corporation members are, they can be found at the county courthouse. I doubt if anyone will ever bother to find out. I think they will just think they are from Linksfort and let it go at that, or if they want to, they can go over and look. I could care less. No one has money to fight it or money to buy us out. At least I don't think so. No, I don't think so.There would be financial sheets each month, telling how much is sold and everything necessary to the business. I know Bob Clark has a son, Hank, who would be very good at managing the feed mill. Parley, who now manages the hardware store would be good to keep there. He also had no time for the Pattons I found out this past week."

"And the creamery?" Ted asked.

"They have a good manager there now, but he is a Patton man. He's a good friend of the undertaker who you know is Ray and Joe Patton's first cousin. I would like to see him removed, fired, if you like that word better. And I can see you all do. There is another man there, name of Paul Denton that would be good. He has worked there for a long time and as I understand has done a great deal of the managing, although the manager got all the credit. There is a great deal of panic in Casson now. When are the businesses to be sold? Who will own them? And will I have a job? All but Pearson at the creamery. He thinks he's secure."

"It appeals to me," Addy told him. "Very much. Even more than owning that land, although that I would like too. I have ugly, hard feelings for the town of Casson. I know the Pattons had a lot to do with our being shoved out of that town, but still there are people who did not want Martin to come to town because of his sickness, nor did they want any of his family. It was just like the sickness was going to rub off on them because we carried it too. I want to think about this. I want to talk about this with everyone here. Think a lot and talk a lot. We have to look at our books again. Do a lot of thinking," Addy told him.

"I understand. All three of these come up on the sheriff's auction the fifteen of November. That gives three weeks. The ranches come up for sale the same day."

"What happens if no one can buy any of the ranches?" Ted asked.

"I understand the government will buy them. The government is buying land, gumbo, all over the place for anywhere from a dollar and a half to three dollars an acre. Cheap. Marginal land north and east of town is going for four to eight dollars an acre."

"Who runs it then?" Linc asked.

"They put in renters. I suppose when there is money again the land will be sold back. I don't think the government is going to stay in the ranching business any longer than they have to. I will be waiting to hear from you, say in two weeks time because I have to get hold of Walter Talor and set up this corporation. I think this can be done without anyone knowing who put the money into it. And when the time comes, then it can be told. Until then, it's no one else's business. How many sections are in these ranches?"

"Boyen and Clark's has a section and a half, I think. That

would be 960 acres. And the government is buying land like that for a dollar and a half to three dollars an acre?" Linc asked.

"Both ranches should go for a lot more, but I don't know who has money to buy them. That's one thousand three hundred and eighty two dollars at a dollar and a half an acre. And two thousand eight hundred and eighty dollars at three dollars an acre for Boyen and Clark's."

"Clinton has a section. And at a dollar and a half an acre that would be nine hundred sixty and at three dollars an acre it would be one thousand nine hundred twenty dollars," Ted told them.

"A lot of money when no one has any," Lay said.

"You never said who else was in this corporation," Annie told him.

"I forgot. I have to do that so you know who else would be in this. I am one, Leo Arnold is another one. Do you know him? He has a large ranch on the other side of Casson."

"I do," Addy answered. "He used to be a friend of Martin's when they were kids. His folks lived near Martin's folks. You remember him, don't you Linc? He is short, quite bald, slight man, hard working. Martin always liked him." Linc nodded his head yes.

"Which is his reason for putting into this corporation, cause he felt Martin and his people had been crucified by the Patton's. The third party is Tom Raymer, Casson's mayor and the Allis Chalmers implement dealer here in Casson. He has a going hatred of Ray and Joe Patton. He never said anything or made like he didn't like them cause they could have put him out of business, but he has an intense hatred of both brothers, especially Joe."

"I remember Raymer," Addy said. His wife died about the time I married Martin. I remember the first time I saw him in church, I asked Martin who he was because he looked so distinguished and eloquent," she said as she saw Annie raise her eyebrows. "I asked Martin who he was and he said he was the mayor in town. And I thought that he looked just like he should be that. Nice looking tall man, slightly heavy, but still eloquent," she repeated as she saw Annie smile broadly adding, "That is an interesting lot. We'll have to get back to you within a few days. This will take some thinking and talking about."

"Just let me know shortly so everything can be written up," Lay said putting on his lightweight jacket. "I hope you can see your way to joining us in this venture. I feel it is a worthwhile one, just a way of getting our feet into that town and hopefully, in time, seeing it go the right way."

Time was spent counting the money they had stashed away in the coffee cans that were buried here and there under boards in the various buildings. Along with the inheritance Addy had left, they totaled five thousand four hundred dollars and fifty-four cents.

"If anyone knew what we have here," Addy said, "our lives would not be worth anything."

"No, we'd be killed," Linc agreed. "You won't have much inheritance left, Addy. I don't like that at all. Course it depends on what we end up paying."

"It was always a good feeling to know there was money in the cans if we had to have it. And always a good feeling to be able to add to that money. A little once in a while," Ted said.

"I know all that. I have almost four thousand dollars left of the inheritance. We've stretched that inheritance a long ways. We used some here in the house to fix the kitchen. Martin put a new roof on the house and also new siding. It needed it so badly. And then buying High Ranch and Big Mile Ranch took a lot. But I've never been sorry about buying either of them. Land has always been a good investment," Addy replied.

"Well, we've hashed this over and over," Linc said. "There has to be a decision made. We have steers going to the meat market every month so there is money coming in, not a lot, but a little. We have our tax money saved out. That was not counted in. If we wanted to do it, I think we could make it good the rest of the winter and next summer too. By being careful, even more than now, we would have money saved by next fall."

"Course, we don't want to have many problems or we could be in trouble," Ted told them.

"Let's make the decision," Addy said. "Let's go for it, do it. Two thousand dollars for the corporation and as much land as we have money for. You know, we really are trusting people. I think of that again and again. But Lay comes so highly recommended from everyone."

"And none of them like the Pattons," Annie added.

"No. They don't. Give them a plus for that. Ted, you and Linc, go and talk to Lay tomorrow. First thing in the morning."

"I wonder what Pa would say to all of this," Ted pondered.

"If he had been well, we wouldn't have had to do all this," Addy answered.

The fifteenth day of November, a cold blustery day, the family anxiously awaited word from Talor. The sheriff's sale started promptly at nine o'clock in the morning.

"It will be cold standing around that courthouse," Ted commented at breakfast that morning.

"I imagine Talor will be dressed warmly. I studied all the papers that were drawn up on the Prairie Land Corporation again last night," Addy told him.

"You slept good I take it?" Ted asked, raising an eyebrow as he smiled.

"No. I thought I lost all of my religion when we left Casson, but I found that I have a little left. I did some praying. A lot of thinking and lots and lots of not being able to sleep in the past two weeks. Land buying, that I understand, and we are in control of that. But this other, we are not in control of this. We do not understand the operating of those businesses and we sure hope Lay and Talor know what they are doing. Because we could be out a lot of money if they don't."

"My thinking exactly, Addy," Ted agreed finishing his

coffee. "Maybe by noon we'll know."

And by noon they did know that the corporation now owned a hardware store, a feed mill and a creamery. The hardware store and the contents sold for nine hundred dollars. The feed mill sold for two thousand eight hundred dollars and the creamery for two thousand seven hundred fifty dollars.

"The corporation has money left," Talor told them. "There is one thousand five hundred and fifty dollars left. There was only the government as a bidder for the ranches, so you did get both ranches. Bought one for two dollars an acre and one for less because the buildings were gone. Boyen and Clark's went for one thousand nine hundred twenty dollars and Clintons for two thousand eight hundred eighty dollars."

"Were Clinton, Boyen or Clark there?" Addy asked.

"I heard someone behind me say that they didn't see any of them. They thought they had left town, gone somewhere else. Didn't want to stay and see the selling of their land," Talor answered. "Now before I left Casson, I fired Pearson in the creamery and put Paul Denton in as manager. I told him I wanted a complete inventory of the contents before the end of next week. Bob Clark is going to help his son, Hank, in the feed mill, at least for a while. Parley will continue as manager of the hardware store. Both Clarks and Parley are also to do inventory. He wondered, Parley that is, about a name for the hardware store. I told him to call it Casson's Hardware Store. It already is Casson's Creamery and Casson's Feed Mill so I figured that would do for names," grinning he added, "I feel like I've done a good day's work. I hope you all feel the same."

"I'll tell you in a year how good today was," was Addy's wry reply. "Say, I have often wondered, but never thought to ask if anyone knows what happened to Ray and Joe's families now that the men are gone. And is Ruth Patton still going to marry Clinton's son?"

"I guess Ray's wife was so ashamed and shocked at what Ray did, besides not having money left, that she just left town, quiet like. I heard today that she told the lawyer to sell the house and send her the money. Who knows how long that will take and they thought that was all she had for money. Joe's wife and Ray's wife were cousins. From different towns, but both from somewhere west of here in Colorado. She has left too. Her family came down for the funeral and helped her clean out the house, from what I heard today. Daughter Ruth, according to what I heard, has left with the Clintons. She stayed here long enough for the funeral, then told Mama good-bye and Clinton's son drove into town and picked her up and they left together. Not married or anything. Maybe are by now, and I take it Mama was not happy about that either, but Ruth left anyway. That's another reason her family helped her pack up the stuff in the house and helped move her out of town. Such a respectable family and then the daughter leaves town, not married, with her boyfriend."

"Well, well. Even they have to have scandals too," Addy said, then added, "and so the town is rid of two complete Patton families, Ray's and Joe's."

"And for better or for worse," Linc added, "We are now back in Casson. Well, we've got a foothold back in that town anyway."

CHAPTER VII

"Ma," Annie said one afternoon the middle of November. "I would like to have my baby at home this time."

"Well, I had you at home, Ken and Pete too. What does Linc have to say to this?"

"He would like to have a doctor here, but it is a long ways for a doctor to come from Linksfort and we have no telephone to call him. I'd like to stay home. All he did was look at me once in a while and be there when Sara finally came. It takes hours before the baby comes. Anyway, I never even went to the doctor once since I got pregnant this time."

"I know you didn't. It took hours with Sara, but this one might not take so long," Addy answered. "I guess you and Linc will have to make up your mind what to do. It's up to both of you what you want to do. But you'd better make up your mind before long cause you've only got about two weeks before the baby is due to be born."

"I know. Guess we'll have to decide tonight. If I stayed home, I'd like to have Lillian come. She was a nurse and I'd feel good about her being here."

"Does she know that?"

"No. If that is what we decide then we'd have to go and talk to her."

The decision was taken out of their hands when later that night, Annie got her first labor pains.

"Addy," Linc said carrying Sara into the big house. "I don't know if I can get Annie to Linksfort. She's really got bad pains already, coming hard and real close. I think you should come down and see what you think."

"Ma," Annie cried, as Addy came into the room, "I don't want to ride all the way to Linksfort."

"You are having hard pains already and you just got sick about three-fourths of an hour ago? I wasn't with you when Sara was born, so I don't know how long you had pains this hard before she came."

"Oh," Annie cried, grabbing hold of Addy's hands as another pain washed through her.

"Linc," Addy said, "you go get Lillian Barlow. She was a nurse and I sure am not. I'll stay here. You go quick."

"How long will it take him, Ma?" Annie asked.

"I would guess about an hour. Just be glad the roads are good yet. Or he'd have had to go by horse. So much quicker in a car."

Pain after pain washed through her body as Addy held her hands tightly.

"It's a good thing women forget about this pain afterwards," she murmured. "Otherwise there wouldn't be so many babies in this world."

An hour later Lillian hurried into the bedroom as Annie was going into the final minutes of the delivery.

"You want me to leave?" Linc asked.

"Not unless you want to," Lillian answered. "I never could see anything wrong with a man seeing his baby being born. You see other animals born, why not a baby? Now Annie, just a couple more pushes and this will be all over. Good girl," she coaxed until with one final last push, Lillian held the new baby in her hands.

"A boy. You've got a son, Annie, Linc. Looks like a real nice baby too. Here Grandma, you take your grandson while I help Annie finish this up."

An hour later, Annie held her new son in her arms. Addy had washed him, dressed him and put him in Annie's arms.

"What you going to name him?" Lillian asked.

"Seth Lincoln," Annie answered.

"That is a lovely name. I guess you don't call boy's names lovely, but I do like it."

"If he was going to be baptized, I'd have you be his godmother," Annie told her.

"Lands sakes, child. I ain't been to church for so many years that I don't remember how it even goes anymore. I don't think you'd want me," Lillian answered, pleased to be honored in this matter. "Well, Linc, I think you should take me home now. There isn't anything more I can do here."

"I didn't think to make any coffee," Addy told her. "If you want, I'll make some."

"No! No! I just want to go back to my bed for what's left of the night. That coffee can be next time."

"And thanks so much, so very much," Annie told her.

"You're very welcome. Glad I could be of help," was the reply.

With December came the cold weather of winter. The family could see Martin's health deteriorating to a lower level. He had almost completely lost his sense of balance. He was even more bewildered, never knowing where he was. Many hours were spent sleeping during the day. Not daring to chance his getting outside, Addy still kept his bedroom door locked at all times.

The biggest change she realized was his acceptance of her help. The objection and fighting over changing his clothes was not there. He did not object to being bathed or to having his hair washed. His beard, mustache and hair were now kept trimmed. With his becoming docile had also come his inability to feed himself. Making sure his food was soft, Addy always fed Martin before the others came in to eat. She soon learned that when he was full, he just didn't swallow any more and let the food roll out of his mouth. After enough times spent cleaning him up and cleaning up the floor, she learned to fix smaller amounts for him. Broth soaked up with bread, mashed potatoes and gravy, corn bread soaked in milk and cooked cereal became his general diet.

Evie continued to teach the boys. Although it rankled that Rafferty taxes helped support the school district, Addy knew her boys were receiving a much better education. And Addy also had to admit, it was easier as there was not worry about getting the boys to school day after day, even with them riding horseback. The only thing that was bad was their lack of companionship with others their own age. And Addy missed the companionship of the neighborhood, the school parties, the Christmas program, the visiting and the togetherness that used to be.

Christmas came and went. The new year did not look good financially as the depression years were still upon the whole country.

"We are better off than most," Addy told the family as they talked on New Years Day.

"One very good reason is your inheritance and also Pa's being so scared of his sister taking away the ranch from us after his death that he got it all sold to you," Linc commented.

"And for that I've been thankful for so long. And your Sara and now little Seth. They are so nice. Such good babies. Got to be thankful for that."

"And another good thing about this coming year just could be Nellie," Linc joked as he grinned at Ted.

"I am lucky I came to my senses and quit Ruth," Ted said smiling broadly. "I guess it wouldn't have made any difference if I hadn't cause her old man gave me the heave-ho anyway."

"And I suppose we have to be thankful for Martin's not fighting us anymore. At least now he is easier to handle. I can wash him and change his clothes without having to have help getting them off and back on again."

"But a lot of washing now, Ma," Annie told her softly, squeezing Addy's hand.

"Yes, from a man to a child, from a husband and a friend to a baby," Addy answered, wiping the sudden tears from her cheeks.

"And you're only forty-three years old," Linc told her.

She shrugged, "What can I do about it. He would have taken care of me," and they all agreed.

In February there was a fire in the new chicken coop. Hearing a noise in the coop on his way to the barn in the morning, Ted went to investigate. Taking a match from his pocket, he tried to light the lantern hanging inside the door. With the first match he didn't get the wick to light. Again he tried and when it started to burn, he raised the match to his lips to blow it out and lost it. The match fell into the straw at this feet. In just a few seconds the dry straw around him was burning. Grabbing the chicken waterer he dumped the water on the straw, only to find it wasn't enough to contain the flames. By then the fire was dancing in front of the door and Ted knew he had to find another way out. Again taking the empty chicken waterer he crashed it against one of the windows. He found he had to smash the waterer against the window several more times to get a large enough hole so he could crawl through. By this time, the straw was burning all around his feet. Running to the barn he shouted for help. His cries carried, not only to the barn, but also to the house where Addy was taking care of Martin. The ritual was far enough that he had been bathed and had fresh clothes on. She had just heated his breakfast ready to feed him when Ted's cries chased her to the door.

Seeing the chicken coop in flames, Addy grabbed a jacket and ran out into the yard. By this time, the barn crew were running toward the burning building.

"No use, Ted, it's just going to burn. Can't save that

when it's burning so hard," Linc told him.

"Damn, we've lost all our chickens and the new coop."

"How did it start anyway?" Linc asked.

"I heard something in there, and so I went to find out what it was. I lit the lantern but when I tried to blow the match out, it fell into the straw. I tried to put it out with the water in the waterer but there wasn't enough and so I took the waterer and broke the window so I could get out. That straw is so dry that it just went like wild. When I got out the window, half the chicken coop was burning already."

"Nothing we can do here. I'm going back and finish with your pa," Addy told them.

But when she got back in the house, she couldn't find Martin. She scoured the house, finally getting help from the others to hunt for him outside.

"I know he wouldn't put on anything more than he had on when I finished dressing him. He isn't dressed for this and with not being outside all winter, he won't be ready to face that cold," Addy sobbed as she told them.

"We'll look for him. You're sure he's not in the house?" Linc asked.

"Maybe in the cellar," Ken offered.

"No, he couldn't get the trap door open," Addy answered.

"We'll finish the chores after we find Pa," Ted said as they all went toward the house. "Ken, you stay by the chicken coop. Keep an eye on that fire."

By now there was enough light outside that they could see where Martin had stumbled off one side of the porch and had fallen into the snow.

"Oh, he's going to be so cold," Addy wept. "We've got to find him."

"It shouldn't be too hard cause we can just follow his trail," Linc said.

"He's got about ten minutes start on us," Ted said. "Linc, you watch on that side and Pete you watch on this side. Damn, we've lost his trail now. I can't tell where he went."

"He seemed to heading toward the river so I'll look down around here," Linc said.

"Addy, you find anything?" Ted called.

"No, I don't see anything over here. He's going to be so cold. So cold," she cried as she searched.

"I see something down on the river, Addy," Linc called. "Ted, come here and help me down the bank. Damn, it's so full of snow that I can't keep my balance. Yes, Addy, it's Pa. He fell just like I did. We'll never get him back up the way I got down."

"Pete, run and get a rope. And be quick about it," Ted told him. "So much snow down there, Linc?'

"Much that we'll have to drag Pa back up the bank and its so steep here."

"How cold is he, Linc?" Addy asked her teeth chattering from the cold and the tension.

"Cold, Addy. Cold."

"Here is Pete now. We'll hang onto this end and pull you and Pa up."

"I'll have to tie the rope around him and you just pull him up first. The bank here is so steep and I can't carry him and hang onto the rope too. There, now just pull him up." Slowly, Martin was pulled up the bank. Getting him to the top, they flung the end of the rope back down to Linc and helped him back up the bank. When Linc was safely on top, Ted picked up his pa and carried him back to the house.

"Here, Ted. Put him on this chair and help me get off his wet clothes. Oh Martin, I should never have left you alone."

"Addy, don't start to blame yourself. You only did what anyone would do, to go and see what the shouting was about," Linc told her. "And just be glad Ted didn't burn up in that building too. I hope Ken is making out alright. We don't need him burnt either."

Getting the shivering man out of the wet clothes, Addy took a dry towel and started to rub him down, trying to get some warmth into his cold skin.

"Pete, run upstairs and get all the soapstones and put them in that reservoir on the stove. When they get warm we'll put them in his bed and try to warm him up that way. After I rub him down as best I can."

Within a few minutes they had Martin tucked into his bed, two warm soapstones by his feet and several more around the middle of his body. Addy did little more that day but stay with the man. Often taking the soapstones and warming them again, she finally got him to stop shivering and lay warm. Now her biggest worry was pneumonia.

And by the next morning, that fear was real. Martin had a raging fever and a racking cough. And looking outside, Addy knew there was no way that anyone could get a doctor for him. During the night, a raging blizzard had enveloped the prairie, with drifts already piled high around the windows of the house. She knew Stubby or Evie wouldn't be down today. It was not safe to leave the security of the one's own ranch yard. "And I've got such a sick, sick man here," she said to herself.

The storm raged for another day. The wind packed the snow into hard deep drifts. Doing chores was almost more than two men and two boys could get done. Finally they opened the fence around several hay stacks so the cattle could get feed.

Each day it got harder for Martin to breathe. Coughing spells racked his body. Addy stayed by his side day and night, doing whatever she could to ease his pneumonia racked body. She heated goose grease, smeared it on his chest and lay a warm towel on top of the grease. She tried to get him to drink warm water laced with brandy and sugar, but found she could not get this down him.

When the blizzard was over, Ted, Linc, and the two boys worked unceasingly to get the road cleared. Guessing it was only a matter of time before Martin died, they wanted to be able to get to the main highway.

"Where you gonna bury Pa, Addy?" Linc asked one of the evenings.

"I wonder if Pearson will even allow Martin to lay by your ma," she asked.

"There is still bitterness in Casson about us and I know the undertaker is a cousin of Pattons. I don't know if he would take care of Pa or not."

"The room is there for Martin beside your ma's grave. That lot had room for both your grandparents, your ma, your pa, and two other people. It would be a shame if he couldn't be laid to rest beside her. That's the way it's supposed to be."

"After Pa dies, Ted and I'll go to Casson and talk to him. I don't want you to go. You got it hard enough now and you don't have to go through any more. If he won't take care of Pa, then we'll just go to Linksfort. There is a nice cemetery there. I won't beg for anything, Addy."

"No, I know that."

"We've got the road about half cleared out. I never seen anything like this before, never," Linc told her.

"And it had to come now. Right now when we got so much else to handle without that too."

"Well one thing for sure, it don't leave any time to worry about things we can't do nothing about anyway. How much longer do you think Pa will live, Addy?" Ted asked.

"I don't know. His body is full of cold and pneumonia, but his heart has to be strong or he'd have died before now. And that cough is so bad. I hate to hear him start, cause it's so hard for him to stop. His chest has to be so full. He can't hardly get air in it."

"We should have the road cleared by tomorrow, Saturday or Sunday at the latest. After all of this is over, then we'll have to find somewhere to buy a few old hens too. You got to be about out of eggs," Ted said.

"I've been real stingy with using them. Got a few left for another couple of days.

"If I hadn't been so clumsy that morning, this wouldn't have happened," Ted said.

"Ted, I've been through this again and again, and I've finally decided to live with the idea that this is the way it was meant to be. That the fire was meant to be, that Martin's getting so cold and wet was meant to be, and that his dying was meant to be. Don't blame yourself cause then I've got to blame myself too."

"All right Addy, I'll just leave it be. I wonder where we'll ever be able to get a few hens when we do find a place for them," Ted answered.

"Maybe get a few from Andersons and a few from Barlow or over at Linksfort somewhere. Just enough for a few eggs. Didn't get any canned this winter either. Maybe someone will have some we can buy to butcher. Have to see. Maybe ask at the feed mill at Linksfort. I've got recipes that don't use eggs and I know Evie has too. We'll get by. Evie will give me a few eggs too so that will help."

"Addy, you sleep for a couple of hours and I'll stay with Pa," Ted told her. "You're so tired you can hardly keep your eyes open."

"I don't know if I could sleep."

"Try. I'll stay with Pa and if it looks like something will happen I'll get you right away."

It was exactly a week after the fire that Martin died. Curled up on the end of the mattress, Addy suddenly realized she didn't hear any struggling to breathe and she knew the end had come. Curling up in a tight ball, she wept until there were no more tears.

When Ted came in from chores, she met him at the door with the news and asked him to tell Linc. Knowing Barlows had a telephone, they rode horses there and called the undertaker at Casson.

The body could be buried in the cemetery lot, provided they dug the hole. But no, he would not take care of Martin. He would not even consider touching him. So another call to Linksfort brought an undertaker for Martin's body. Late Monday afternoon, the hearse brought the body back to the house where it lay until Tuesday morning.

Monday evening, after everyone had gone to bed, Addy stood by the coffin looking down at the body of the man she had married and loved. Laid out in his wedding suit with his best white shirt and tie, Martin looked peaceful.

"You were a good man," Addy murmured. "Good to me and Annie, good to your family and good to your land and animals. You couldn't help it you got sick. How I wish you could be buried from church, but that is not to be."

She lay her hand on his cold, still hands and bending down she kissed his cheek, saying her final good-bye to her beloved Martin.

The next morning the only friends at the house were Stubby and Evie. Although the family knew Anderson's would have come if they could have, they were buried in deep snow drifts. Having ridden to Barlows, Linc and Ted had told them not to try to come.

The family and the undertaker said a few prayers and then the casket was closed for the final time.

The short funeral procession to the cemetery was three vehicles: the hearse, and the two cars of the Rafferty's. After the casket had been lowered into the hole dug by Linc and Ted Monday morning, Addy watched as Ted, Linc, Pete and Ken shoveled the frozen dirt back into the hole.

"It is over," she said turning once more to look at the brown dirt in the sea of snow. "It is over."

"Some day, some day the people in Casson are going to regret the treatment we have gotten and especially this," Addy vowed on her way back home. "I am so glad the corporation bought that stuff in Casson. I wonder when we will have the opportunity to buy some more, like the funeral home. There is nothing I would like better than to throw him out on his ear."

Stubby and Evie, left at home, had their own problems. He had asked her to help pull a calf. One of the milk cows they kept just for house milk had a problem calving. Knowing he couldn't get the calf pulled by himself, Stubby had asked Evie to assist him.

"Got it done, Evie," Stubby told her as they watched the cow start to lick the calf clean.

"I'm going back to the house. Got bread raising and it should be ready to pan." Opening the barn door, Evie called back to Stubby. "There are two strange horses by the house. I don't like that and I can't see anyone either. You come back with me."

"What if they are stealing or going through the house?"

Evie asked as they walked quickly to the house.

"There is a gun inside the front kitchen door. I'll try to get that on my way in," Stubby answered. Quickly and quietly he opened the door. Grabbing the gun and inserting a shell, he had it ready to fire. Evie, right behind him, had picked up a baseball bat. Listening, they picked up the sound of dresser drawers being pulled out coming from Martin's bedroom. Quietly tiptoeing to the door, they could see two men going through the drawers, pulling them and dumping them onto the floor.

"Get out of there now," Stubby shouted.

"We've got to get out of here," one of the them shouted to the other.

"He's got a gun," the other said, running to the door. Knocking Stubby aside they continued to run across the room to the kitchen door. Evie swung her bat and knocked one down at the same time Stubby fired at the other one, shooting off his hat.

"Got to get out of here," one of them shouted again as they opened the kitchen door and ran to their horses. A quick minute and the horses were galloping out of the yard.

"Well, we've got their hats," Evie said, picking up one of them. "And I wonder if one of them knows how lucky he was that you got the top of his hat instead of the back of his head with that shot. You put a hole in the kitchen wall, anyway."

"Those were kids, Evie. Not men. They couldn't have been even eighteen. I suppose they thought everyone had gone to the funeral and so they would have a while to go through the house."

"Not many people knew Martin had died," Evie said.

"The phone call from Barlows on the party line told everyone that he had died," Stubby reminded her. "You always hear when someone is calling the operator and anyway, how long does it take for news like that to travel. Maybe the undertaker at Casson told it too, like how smart he was to tell the Rafferty's that they couldn't bring their pa in there to be taken care of. News like that travels. I could use a cup of coffee, if there is any, Evie. I don't think they found any money. I don't think they keep it laying around like that," Stubby said. "I am glad you were in the barn with me or else you'd have been up here alone."

"Maybe then they wouldn't have come in at all when they found the house wasn't empty," Evie answered.

"Maybe, cause they sure were not very old. Rafferty's should be back here by noon."

Shortly before noon, the two cars drove into the yard. All came into the house to eat the meal Evie had waiting for them.

"Smells good in here," Ted said. "Got coffee for us right away, Evie? Cow have her calf?"

"Yeah, she did. And damn good thing both of us were here this morning too."

"Why?" Addy asked.

"I had to get Evie to help me pull that calf and then we both came back to the house and routed out two young kids ransacking through Martin's drawers and dressers."

"I suppose they thought we all were gone to the funeral," Addy said.

"Sure looks like it," Stubby answered.

"Know who they were?" Linc asked.

"No. Young. Maybe sixteen or seventeen, maybe eighteen. But young. We got their hats."

"Their hats?" Annie asked getting Sara settled on a chair ready to eat.

"Yep, Evie knocked one down with a baseball bat and I shot at one and knocked off his hat. They left in a big hurry. Addy, guess I put a hole in the wall above the door, kitchen door." He pointed while the rest looked.

"I'm so glad you both are alright," Addy said shuddering.

"We made it a policy a long time ago not to leave this place alone and we almost blew it today. If it hadn't been for that cow calving we would have had you two come with us. Now I am so glad we didn't. Evidently, these were not two experienced robbers, just kids trying to pick up a few extra bucks."

"They picked out a poor place to hunt for money. I never left any in there cause I didn't know what Martin would have done with it. Only his clothes were in there," Addy said.

"Well, one thing for certain. This is a lesson never to be forgotten. We never leave this place alone and we make sure two people, adults are here at all times. And a man with the women if possible. We were lucky. It could have been much worse," Ted said. "What we going to do for a chicken coop and for laying hens?"

"I think we could use that one larger calf pen in the barn for now. Have to put some kind of chicken netting over it to keep them in, but it would do for now until spring when we'll have to do something else," Linc answered. "There are two smaller buildings that wouldn't be too hard to move from High Ranch that we could use for chicken coops if we could move them down here. If we used a hay wagon we could move them I think."

"I think we could move them too," Ted agreed. "We could use part of one for putting feed in and then it wouldn't be so hard to feed them in the winter time. But we need laying hens now and who knows where we're going to find them."

"Ask at the mill next time you go. Maybe they know where to find some. Evie will give us a few eggs to help out for making noodles and dumplings and that sort of thing," Addy told them. "If we could get a half dozen hens from this one and some from another, and a few from someone else until we have about two dozen, we'd be alright for the rest of the winter. I wish we could pick up a few to butcher too, while we're at it."

"Next time we're in town we'll see what we can do about it," Linc agreed. "In the meantime we'll fix up that pen in the barn for hens and in the spring we'll have to move those buildings down and get them fixed up."

By the time it was all finished, they had three dozen laying hens, and twenty hens for butchering. Bob Clark at the feed mill knew a rancher that was low on feed and was willing to sell the Rafferty's some chickens. After moving them they tested them to see how many were laying eggs. The ones not laying were butchered and canned for summer time eating.

"You want help putting that bed back into the bedroom?" Ted asked the morning after the funeral.

"I'm not going to do anything with that room until spring. I've been thinking of painting it. Really clean it good, just do it up good. You and Linc should divide up Pa's clothes."

"Linc don't know if he wants any of them," Ted answered.

"That's silly. Pa would have wanted his boys to wear them out. There are those overalls I got him for Christmas that are just like new and socks are the same. Just like new."

"I'll see what Linc says this morning."

"And there are lots of papers in that one dresser of his in the corner. I have never gone through them. Maybe we can do that this afternoon if you and Linc have time. I don't think there is anything in there that Annie needs to be here for. Sara sleeps in the afternoon and lots of times the baby does too. She gets some things done when they are both laid down."

"You're going to clean up that room before you move back in there?" Linc asked Addy that afternoon.

"Yes, I would feel better if I could leave the window open for a while and it has to be warm when that is done. I got a place to sleep now. The room smells and the mattress has to be burned up. It's straw so it should burn good. I'll make another one this coming fall when we have fresh straw. I'm glad you got those clothes divided up and the rest will be burnt in the stove. Now let's get those dresser drawers out here and go through them."

"These are papers from the ranch here when Pa bought it. And here is some from the time when his pa died and he had to get a lawyer to straighten out the mess with his sisters over the ranch. They are all here," Ted said.

"Those we have to save," Linc answered. "I wonder how long it will be before news of Pa's death sifts down to them. They live far enough away that it may take awhile. And we don't exchange letters with them after that happened. Pa wouldn't write to them."

"They don't talk, ever since that day," Ted said. "Aunt Ella said she would never speak to Pa again, but when he died, she'd get that ranch back and sell it and get the money her Ma wanted her to have. I remember those words clearly."

"Pa said his ma babied that one sister so much that she just felt she should have everything. It was her right."

"These are old receipts from feed and that sort of thing. I think we'll just pack them into a box and put them in the attic," Addy commented. "But what's here, way down in the back of this small drawer?"

"What did you find, Addy?" Linc asked.

"An envelope with a key in it. It's from the Linksfort National Bank, dated 1903 on the envelope."

"That's the year I was born," Linc said.

"I wonder what it's for?" Ted asked.

"It's from a lockbox," Addy answered. "Your pa never mentioned anything about this. Did he know anyone in Linksfort?"

"Pa had a cousin that lived in Linksfort that he was real close to. He looked a lot like Pa. He never married, died before you and Pa married."

"Well, the rest of this is just things that can be thrown away. Some of this we'll put upstairs in the attic, some of this should go into a lockbox, like the agreement that was drawn up with the Martin's sisters so we have a good copy of that just in case they ever drive in here. And we should put the real estate transfers in the lockbox too. We kept them here at home cause we felt better, but I think Dave Lay's bank is a good one. Maybe it would be a better place to keep them than here in this dresser drawer," Addy told them.

"And when we go to town next time we'll go into the bank and see if this here key is any good anymore. And if it is, what's in the lockbox?" Ted wondered.

The following week, Ted and Linc did go to town and to the Linksfort National Bank.

"What brings you in town today?" Dave asked shaking their hands. "It is nice to see you. Come on into my office and take a few minutes to visit with me. Catch up on the news."

"Dave, when we cleaned out Pa's papers we came upon this key for a lockbox here in this bank. We came to check it out."

"Don't lockboxes have rent paid on them to keep them from year to year?" Linc asked.

"Yes. But sometimes the rental is taken out of the account. That's what has happened to the one you brought the key in for. I know which lockbox it is because it's been here long before I came and the rental was always taken out of the account. Made out that way."

"Now I am curious. Let's go see what's in it," Ted urged.

"I'll go with you to open it up. And then you can go through it in private and take whatever you want out to take home."

"You said there is money in an account to pay for it?" Linc asked.

"Yes," Dave answered. "Here is the box. Go in here and you are by yourselves."

"We got some stuff, papers here, that need to be put into a lockbox. Thought we'd rent one today," Linc told him.

"All right. I'll get one of the clerks to get it ready for you. Big one by the looks of all that you are carrying."

"There is a savings book in here and a letter," Ted said after Lay left them.

"This here saving book is made out to Lincoln and Theodore Rafferty," Linc told him.

"What's in the letter?" Ted asked.

"Dear Lincoln and Theodore," Linc read after he opened the envelope. "Although I hope to be able to tell you about this savings account myself, if something should happen to me I am going to write this letter that will explain everything.

I have a key to this box and I have given one to your pa. I told him this savings account was to be given to you Lincoln when you were thirty years old and you, Theodore when you are twenty nine years old. It was to be divided evenly between both of you.

This account was started the day you, Lincoln, were born. I started it with a $100.00 deposit and added twenty dollars every month to it. When you, Theodore were born I added another $100.00 dollars to it and every month from then on I added forty dollars so there was twenty dollars for each of you. There were months when I put in a smaller amount or nothing if I found I was short of money that month or something came up I had to pay on before this.

I felt by the time you were thirty and twenty-nine years old, both of you would be settled and not throw away this money. You see, I loved your ma. I loved her from the first time I saw her. She was then eighteen years old. But she loved your pa and never ever thought of me as anything but Martin's cousin. I knew I would never marry if I could not marry her. So in a way, I felt you two boys were like my own sons, the ones I would never have. There was no way I could marry any other woman regardless of how much everyone thought I should get married.

Kind thoughts and regards to both of you.

And it is signed Lincoln Rafferty."

"Well I'll be damned," Ted said, shaking his head in disbelief.

"When is the last deposit made?" Linc asked.

"January, 1917. Can't read the exact date cause it is smeared.

"I was fourteen years old," Linc said, adding "That was when he died. I remember Pa and Ma going to his funeral. I remember that very well."

"So do I cause that's when Ma caught a cold that went into pneumonia and she died right after that. Let's go to

Dave and find out how much money there is here now, cause with interest it will be more than it shows here."

"What does it show," Linc asked.

"It shows almost four thousand dollars."

When Dave got a final total for the two men, the savings account showed a total of five thousand six hundred ninety eight dollars and twenty-four cents.

"I want to talk to you in private, Linc," Ted said, walking back into the little room where they had taken the bank box apart. "I don't know about you, but I'd like to take some of this, at least some of my share and give it to Addy to put back into her inheritance can."

"I think that would be a good thing to do. Say about six hundred. That would be three hundred apiece for each of us to give her."

"Let's leave an even five thousand here and take the rest. Then she'll have money to buy paint with or whatever she wants to use some for. Let's think about this just a little more. How about taking some more and putting it into an account here for her.

"Say a thousand?" Linc asked. "Or what did you have in mind?"

"That would leave two thousand for each of us if it were divided. Yes, that sounds good. She has done so much for us that it just seems right," Ted said.

"I'm all for it. Or do you want to think about it some?"

"No. Let's get it done cause with the weather, we don't know when we can get back again. And we'll still have money here in case of trouble, like a fire or a storm or droughts."

"Or funeral parlors coming up for sale," Linc added.

"Six hundred and some bucks is a lot of money to be carrying home. Some on you and some on me and some stashed away somewhere in the car," Ted said. Going back to Dave Lay they told him what they wanted.

"Your bank ain't gonna go under is it?" Linc asked Dave.

"No. Definitely not. We are very solid here. Joe Patton asked for problems there. People come here and ask for loans, we check them out very well. If we do not think they are a good risk, they do not get the money. If one of Patton's friends asked for money or if they could loan money to someone and then control them, the money was loaned. Many times these people could not make even interest payments. Finally the bank got into such a bad situation with too much money loaned out and not enough coming back in that the State Department of Banking came in, and when they found this out, they closed them down. "I am glad to see most of the money left here. It is a good feeling to know this money is here if you ever need it should an emergency come up," Dave answered.

"Or there is something special to buy," Ted laughed. "Like funeral parlors."

"Oh yes, let's not forget that. Still got too many Pattons in that town. You ever find out why they worked so hard to try to get rid of you people?" Dave asked.

"No," was Linc's reply.

"I was told a little of their families history. My wife and I were visiting some friends the other Sunday and one of the other dinner guests was a man and his wife that used to live at Casson, quite a long time ago. He and his wife are older people. He was a minister in one of the churches there. Anyway, he asked about the Casson bank and in the conversation he said that the Patton family were wealthy people. Grandpa Patton married into a family that was also wealthy. When she got older Grandma Patton got sick, something like Martin. They kept her pretty confined in the house so no one really saw much of her, but the hired help talked plenty. After she died, a few years later, Joe and Ray's ma started to act the same as her ma had.

Ray and Joe's pa was so ashamed of her that he bought the ranch where Ray lived to get her out of town cause she wandered all over the streets. After she moved out there, a year or so after, she was trampled by a bull. The rumor was that the old man let her go into the pasture with the bull on purpose and she got killed. The old man's feelings were installed into Ray and Joe from little on. The old man couldn't handle anyone with mental problems and neither could his sons."

"That explains a lot," Linc answered. "A whole lot."

"And so you get rid of someone with any head problems. Just get them to move away so you don't have to look at them cause it might rub off onto you," Ted said.

"And there are still two cousins left there," Dave answered.

"Yes, the undertaker and the postmaster," Linc said.

"Those are the two," Dave answered.

That evening while visiting with Ted and enjoying the last of the strong, hot coffee, Addy's comment was, "Terrible thing, fear. They watched two women, and very important women in their lives, go crazy and the fear of anything like that took away any common sense they ever had. And especially after their pa put that fear into them. You know a pa is necessary to a family, but a ma is more important to a child than anyone. And even when you grow older, like fifteen or so, a ma is still so necessary. And to have them go crazy and then have a pa that hated a crazy woman and put that fear into them really is bad. It sure explains a lot."

"But there are ways to handle that kind of thing, besides what their pa did, Ray and Joe's that is."

"Yes, for sure," Addy answered, "And again, thanks for the money and the savings account." Tears welled in her eyes.

"You're welcome. Say, Linc and I talked while going over there today and we got to get some more hired help. Got to pick up another man somewhere. Ken is still in school and got another year to go and Pete three years to go after this one. With that extra land we bought, we'll have to have help."

"Got any ideas of where to find one we can trust?" Addy asked.

"Going to talk to Stubby about that. He knows a lot of people in Linksfort. We never thought about it after we got to the bank, what with finding that deposit book, but I suppose Dave Lay could have given us names."

Stubby had a possible solution to the problem when they asked him.

"I've got a cousin that needs work. Name is Tony Parker. Works in the sale barn when it runs and picks up whatever he can otherwise. Handyman sort of jobs. There is lots of that kind of work only no one has money to pay you for it. He does pick up a lot of home canning and some chickens to eat and that sort of thing. You do this for me and I'll give you a chicken in payment sort of thing. His wife died a couple of years ago. He's younger than me, about 40 to 45. Got a son that lives near him. The son married, but she got tired of living from hand to mouth so she up and packed her stuff and took off back to where she came from. Left about a year ago. The son works on a ranch near Linksfort."

"Tony probably would be glad for a steady job. He could bunk with us," Evie said.

"Yes, he could stay with us," Stubby agreed. "I wanted to say this a long time now, but never thought it was ever the right time. But Evie and me have so much liked working for you people. You never put on airs. You live thrifty. Clothes are worn out and patched and patched before throwing away."

"And Addy makes rugs out of the pants that can't be worn for good anymore and saves and cooks thrifty and never wastes anything," Evie interrupted.

"I remember Patton, Ray that is, when he drove past on the highway and when he was on his horse, he never even spoke to us and looked down on us like we were poor trash that was beneath him," Stubby told them.

"We like the way you people live. It's the only way we know and we like it. Feel like we fit in," Evie said adding, "You cut buttons off of clothes and save them and use them again. You use string from the store to darn with and make your own soap and had recipes that everybody uses these days in this depression and both of us feel that if you wanted to, you could have bought lots of things that you did without, or you made things here at home that you could have bought. And liver sausage and raw meat sausage you could have bought in the store."

"We felt that if you had money to buy land in these hard years when lots of people don't have money for even a pair of shoes for their kids, then you could have bought lots of things in the stores that you didn't," Stubby told them. "Like buying toothpaste instead of using salt and soda for brushing your teeth just like everybody else does. And using catalogs in the toilet instead of buying that nice soft paper. It's things like that that make us feel at home here, like you are our kind of people."

"I can't see wasting anything," Addy replied. "Sure we had the money to buy those ranches when they came up for sale. But because of the foreclosures they came up cheap, or we couldn't have bought them. We always feel we have to be careful with money cause we don't know when we might have a fire and need money to rebuild what was burnt or have some more dry years like we've been having. Got taxes to pay and on more land now. Just can't see wasting anything. And as for putting on airs, I just can't see any of us acting like that. And I did inherit money."

"Like we said, Evie and me, we like the way you people live. And if you hadn't been careful how you spent money, you wouldn't have had the money to buy that land. You wouldn't have been able to scrape together the money to buy that land. Granted, like Addy said, it was part of her inheritance, but still she could have spent it all wildly and not have had it for what she wanted. Lived high on the hog, you might say," Stubby said.

"I imagine it makes the neighbors and people in Casson wonder," Linc added.

"Let them. You think about it a minute. We don't have many of the old neighbors left anymore, what with ranchers being foreclosed on like they were last fall," Addy said. "Not many left. Things are changing."

"I suppose this summer will see lots of hobo's and tramps again," Evie said. "That is the only thing I don't like about living where our house can be seen from the highway. We've never been bothered yet, but I suppose that will happen yet."

"Maybe too far from the road to walk," Linc said. "You're far enough away that maybe it looks like a long hike."

"Let's hope that continues. I don't want any by my door. Not that I don't feel sorry for them. Most of them would work if they could find a job. Not fun to go hungry or have to wear newspapers on their legs in winter cause they are cold and don't have money to buy warm underwear. Not fun at all," Stubby said, continuing, "Evie and me. We just got lucky. I know it wasn't any fun for your family having neighbors like you did or having Martin so sick. But for Evie and me, well, we just got lucky that you needed us. And we appreciate everything that has happened to us since we came here. We say thank you."

"And you're welcome. Both of you. We were lucky to find you."

Many days Addy forced herself to work. It seemed like she was in a vacuum of emptiness. While Martin was alive, she had a purpose. She had to take care of him. He was always there, needing her. Now he was gone and it seemed like she had lost her reason for living. Maybe, she thought, once spring is here, it will be better. And it was. The days were filled with work so there wasn't time to do so much thinking. The wonder of the new woolly lambs, the fluffy yellow baby chicks, white faced calves looking for their mothers and new born colts filled Addy with pleasure. She spent many warm days helping pick up the yard, doing a yard housecleaning, as Annie put it. After putting it off for weeks, Addy finally decided it was time to tackle Martin's bedroom. The old mattress was taken out and burned, along with the rug that Martin had laid on for so many nights to sleep.

"You sure you want to burn this, Ma?" Annie asked looking at the rug. "It could be washed up and it would be good enough for the upstairs."

"No, there are stains on it that never will come out. I just want it gone." And so it was burned. Ceilings and walls were washed to get rid of the smoky grime that comes from wood burning stoves. Two layers of white paint were applied to the ceiling and then two layers of light green paint to the walls.

"Maybe selfish of me to paint that room when the rest of the house needs painting too," Addy told Annie. "But I wanted it clean before I slept in there again and that was the only way I could get it as clean as I wanted. Now several coats of varnish on the floor and the woodwork, clean windows, freshly ironed curtains, polished furniture and I think I can make it my bedroom again."

"It will look nice, Ma," Annie agreed. "You are making it just your room by doing all this."

"I think I can find enough extra money that I could even paint the upstairs too. I've been thinking about it. I wondered if I should be spending the money for paint right now, but then I thought about it some more and figured I would anyway. The upstairs ain't been painted since I come and I don't know how long before that, so I'm going to do it."

"You're going to keep yourself busy," Annie told her.

"Maybe that's the main reason for doing it, besides it needs it. And I've been thinking too, I think I'm going to learn to drive. Then I can go up to see Jessie Anderson and Lillian Barlow once in a while when the roads are good. I can drive up to Evie's, get her and take her back and drive up on High Ranch and Big Mile Ranch sometimes."

"Ma," Annie answered excitedly, "you really are going to do different things."

"I didn't say I would drive, but I said I've been thinking about it," was the answer. "It's been so different living now without Martin. I never lived here without him before. You were nine years old, Linc was still a boy, and Ted was a year younger than Linc when we got married. Kenny was born two years later and Pete two years after that. I was busy doing a garden, sewing, cooking, and just keeping house. I was happy, mind you. I liked my life. Well, I've still got two boys to finish raising, but it's different now. I just can't seem to get settled again. I'm not happy with the day's work when I go to bed at night. I keep looking for something I just can't seem to find. Something to make things better. Maybe I'm expecting too much too soon. Jessie Anderson said I got to wait a while before I'll be content again. She used the work content and I guess that's a good word. Anyway I think I'm going to learn to drive. Martin's car is here and I think it is time."

And Addy did learn to drive. Linc taught her, at the same time offering to teach Annie, but she felt she had enough to handle with her two youngsters without taking on another project. By the middle of the summer, Addy had her driving license. This gave her freedom she never had before.

The rains during the summer were few and far between. The gumbo cracks could be seen in the ground, getting larger and larger as the days went by without any moisture. Prairie grass started to dry up and the cattle had to hunt for food.

The men could see they were going to get only one cutting of hay so they picked out several areas on the gumbo that had quite a few tumbling tumbleweeds growing on them. By cutting the weeds while they were green, Linc and Ted were able to get more hay for the cattle for the coming winter.

"You be careful making that hay," Annie told Linc as he left one morning to stack hay. "You know how easy it is for that hay loader to pick up rattlesnakes. You're working on that wagon stacking and I hope you see those snakes if they come up with the hay."

"We threw two two yesterday," was his answer as he left.

Coming home late that afternoon, the men told of a fire along the railroad tracks started by the friction of the railroad cars against the tracks.

"It didn't last too long, the fire that is, but I can see where it could be a problem," Linc said. "Stubby said he and Evie rode along the tracks one day and they could see lots of places where fires had started, but along there it is mostly rocks and the ground is so hard that there ain't much to catch fire and burn."

"David said nearer Linksfort there have been more fires and some of them big cause there is lots of brush and tumbling tumbleweeds along the tracks. Said they have had a lot of problems there," Ted said adding, "they had to get a lot of ranchers out with tanks of water and wet gunny sacks to pound down the fire before it got to burning across the open prairie."

"Prairie fires can burn like crazy," Addy agreed. "Hope Stubby and Evie don't have to worry too much about that."

"No," Linc agreed, "None of us need anything like that. Be glad when it starts to rain or when snow comes with enough so it does some good."

"I don't think we'll get much winter wheat this year," Ted said after they checked the wheat one afternoon shortly after that. "We'll be lucky if we get a couple of bushels an acre."

"Barley looks worse than wheat," Linc added. "I don't think we'll get even that much."

"You'll go through the threshing though, won't you?" Addy asked.

"Sure. Cause we need the wheat for flour for one thing and for feeding. Need the straw. May have to feed that too. Good thing for the first cut hay we got and the prairie hay we got. May have to cut down on brood cows this fall. Only keep what really looks good so we have feed enough for them. Got some hay left from last year and that will help. Turn them into the river bottoms when they get home from the prairie. Maybe bring them home early if there ain't anything left and let them go into the bottoms for a while."

"This has to be the poorest year we've had for crops." Addy complained.

"We've got it better than some have," Linc told her. "They said at the mill last week that in Kansas the people plug the holes by the windows in their houses to try to keep the dust out from the dust storms. Terrible there. Just blowing and blowing, and then grasshoppers finishing off what little was left. Stories have it, the grasshoppers were so thick in some areas that they covered fence posts from one end to the other in clusters and clumps. Just ate everything in sight."

"We've got some here, but nothing like that. They done a lot of damage to the prairie grass, what there was left of it," Ted told him.

"Hope they don't get at our garden," Addy said.

"If they did, you wouldn't have anything left," Linc said. "When they come in so thick they just come in clouds, they don't leave anything left. Terrible. Even eat on animals they say, sometimes they eat their eyes right out. So far we've been lucky that way. Not much hay or grass left for the stock, but still better than some are."

"And this was the summer I was going to do such a good job of watching for the chokecherries and the blackberries and gooseberries and wild raspberries. And now they're dried up and we won't get any of them. Last time I really got a lot of fruit was before Martin got sick. The years he was sick I didn't have the time to worry about it and last summer I just didn't seem to care, and now there ain't any. What I had canned is mostly gone," Addy told them.

"There ain't nothing better than canned blackberries thickened and spooned over pancakes or bread toasted on top of the stove," Ted answered.

"We'll have to wait and see what next year brings I guess," Addy replied. "The boys got a dead tree spotted that has a lot of bees around it. They think maybe there is honey in there. I don't know what the poor bees will find to get honey out of either cause everything has dried up. Anyway, later on this fall someone will have to check that tree for them cause the boys think where there are bees, there has to be honey too ."

"Now that would taste really good. I'll go with them and look," Linc volunteered.

"I suppose the apples are smaller on those trees by the

creek too?" Ted asked Addy.

"I looked the other day when I was riding and there seems to be a small crop and small apples, the dry is affecting them too, I suppose. Hope we get enough for drying and some for apple cider too. I haven't made that either since before Martin got sick. This is the year to do all of those things again and now the weather has dried up so much of what I wanted to do."

"We've got the dandelion wine anyway," Ted said. "Nellie hadn't ever tasted dandelion wine or beet wine either. I told her Addy has made each and so she can hardly wait to taste them. Said if she likes it, dandelion wine, she would try to make some next spring."

"We'll have some next time she comes. I had forgot about beet wine. I'll make some of that this fall with the large beets that are too big for anything else. Let some grow extra large," Addy replied.

"And sauerkraut," Linc told her. "I hate that job, but since I really like it with pork, I guess I can help make it too."

"Stubby don't mind helping make it. He stood right there last year and shredded head after head of cabbage. Ken and Pete packed it into the big stone jars. If I remember right neither one of you helped last year."

"Suits me fine. Do it again when the boys can help," Linc told her.

"With the irrigation here, we should have a good garden. And if the grasshoppers keep away, or most of them, then we should have some of the jars full and some vegetables in the basement. I slacked off this past three years with canning and now I may run short before next summer," Addy told them.

"Then we'll just have to eat more milk toast and browned fried potatoes with cream poured over—"

"And," Ted interrupted, "more baked beans and fried cornmeal mush and oatmeal mush fried with honey, if we can find any—"

"And potato soup," Linc added cutting into Ted's sentence.

"I don't think we'll go hungry," Addy agreed. "As long as we have milk and some eggs and meat and vegetables we'll live if we don't get much wild fruit. Save the strawberries for special meals, then, like one of you said, thicken them and have them over pancakes. We have it good compared to those that don't have money to buy shoes for their kids or food for their stomachs. We've got it good. Ain't nobody coming into our basement cellars and taking part of our canning to pay the rent, the canning we had to have so our family had something to eat during the winter. When we complain and feel down in the mouth we had better remember that we will have our stomachs full even if it ain't quite what we would like. We still have it good."

Linc and Ted talked of putting in another dam in the fall on Big Mile Ranch that would be filled with snow in the winter and rain water in the spring so the cattle wouldn't have to go so far to get water each day. Now those cattle on Big Mile Ranch had to go miles to the river, while the cattle on High Ranch had to go to the dam. All were grateful for the dam that was already built when this ranch was bought.

Ted told of seeing pigs running loose east of Linksfort. He had been told there were sows in the woods and along the river bottoms east of Casson. Farmers couldn't get anyone to buy them, and when the feed ran out they just let the animals run loose. Anyone that could catch one could have it to butcher.

"Signs of the time," Stubby told Evie. "Hard times."

CHAPTER VIII

The first days of August, Addy was visited by the new school board. Walter Butman, Albert Cotring and David Barlow. Butman's ranch lay east of Dan Andersons. Cotring was new to the area, having rented the ranch that lay west of High Ranch. Addy had heard David had accepted the presidency of the board when she last drove up to Jessie Andersons.

"We have two things to talk about today," David told her when they were invited in for coffee. "One, we want your boys to come back to school and two, we need your Evie for a teacher."

"So it ain't so much that you want us again in the school, but you need my teacher?" Addy teased with a laugh.

"Now you know all our secrets," David retaliated. "Seriously, it's time you folks were a part of this community again. Everything has changed. There are new people everywhere. The ranch west of me and the one west of the old Boyen and Clark ranch are being rented. The government owns them now. What you call the Boyen and Clark ranch, Addy?"

"River Ranch. Not too original, I guess, but one day someone said the ranch by the river so it stuck."

"That will do, I guess. Anyway, the neighborhood has changed and we want you back. Evie too for a teacher if she wants to."

"You have to talk to her about that. She is home today, didn't come down this morning. She is a good teacher, David. Very good. My boys learned a lot from her."

"We are willing to pay her seventy-five dollars a month," Albert told her.

"That's as good a wage as anyone can get. When it is nice, she can get this far with Stubby when he drives. He drives when the roads are good enough and rides horseback when it's bad. She is an excellent horseback rider. Maybe when the weather looks bad, she can stay here and then it wouldn't be so far for her to get to school."

"Stubby probably wouldn't mind staying there alone some of the time."

"He won't be alone cause his cousin is working for us now and he stays with them. His name is Tony Parker, been here a while now. Good man," Addy answered.

"Then we'll go up and talk to her this afternoon. Got to get this settled cause the teacher we had just told us that he ain't gonna teach this fall. Got offered another job in town and I don't blame him for taking it.

"We'll see you folks at the school cleaning picnic this fall, I hope," Walter told Addy.

"We'll come, I guess," Addy answered. "You know there may be a lot of changes in the neighborhood, but there is still one family that hates us with a passion. And that is Henry Martin. Their family and the Clintons were thick. What with Mark Clinton engaged to Ruth Patton, their dislike for us got even stronger. What are they going to say about us being back in the school?"

"He's got all he can handle at home with that wild son of his. Seems this kid of his, think his name is John, has taken to looting houses, stealing from them while the people were gone. He is in cahoots with a Pete something or other, I can't remember the last name, from somewhere south of here. Don't know the people, but the kid lived with his aunt and uncle, and they ain't worth much either from what I hear. Anyway, this Pete and John Martin got caught and Pete was shot. Didn't die, but got his leg shot-up good. Martin got away, but Pete told the authorities all about what he and Martin were doing."

"How they get caught?" Albert asked.

"The rancher where they were, came home and found them. Didn't take kindly to what they were doing, and shot at them as they ran across the yard to get their horses. Pete was shot good in the leg. Martin got away, but like I said, Pete told what happened and the sheriff came and got young Martin. Charges have been filed against him and he'll go up the river for a while if they are proved."

"Then I guess I won't worry about what he has to say anymore," Addy said. "And what about the Kleetens, the ones that started the fighting in the first place, the time my boys got beat up in school?"

"They moved out when Ray Patton sold his ranch. I think when he moved they felt they lost their support and so they moved. Don't know where and don't care," David answered. "You ain't got to worry about them anymore, Addy," David assured her. "We're going to be on our way. Got to see Evie yet. See you at the schoolhouse the Saturday before Labor Day."

"Now we know who was in our house the day of the funeral," Addy told Ted at supper that night.

"Who?" he asked.

"John Martin, Henry's son and a friend of his, a Pete something-or-other from south of here. The new school board was here today and asked me to send the boys back to school. When I told them that Henry would not welcome us back, David said he had all he could handle at home with that kid of his. He and the other boy were caught stealing in some rancher's house, don't know who. They didn't say who it was. The rancher shot at both of them as they went for their horses. John got away, but the other one got shot in the leg good. He confessed to the whole thing and the sheriff came and got John. David said Henry had all he could handle to take care of that without causing us grief when our boys went back to school. Oh and they want Evie to teach this year as the other teacher got offered a job teaching in town and he took it. Can't blame him, compared to driving back and forth every day. And Kleetens are gone, too."

"Who is the new school board?" Ted asked.

"David, Walter Butman and Albert Cotring. I didn't know Cotring."

"I don't either. Butman I do know. He kind of stayed on the fence throughout our problems with the school and Patton's. He did all his trading in Casson and he just stayed out of everything."

"They were nice here today. Didn't say much about Patton's, but when I mentioned Henry and his hating us, they all said not to worry about him anymore."

"I sure am glad Stubby didn't connect with his shooting at those kids when they broke in here or we'd have been up to our ears again in trouble. It sure would have been Stubby's fault if he had hit that kid. Regardless, it wouldn't have made any difference that they were going through the house here. Sure am glad."

"So am I, I hadn't thought about that at all. I've been thinking about our boys going back to school."

"What are Evie's feelings about teaching there?"

"I haven't talked to her. She was home today and they went up there to see her. I imagine she will accept. Especially when the boys ain't here for her to teach anymore."

Addy knew some of the family had to help with the schoolhouse cleaning. The fear of still being the outcast made her uneasy about that day. It was decided the new hired man, Tony, would stay home and watch over the place. He offered to watch Sara and Seth for Annie, an offer she gladly accepted. Linc would go early with Addy, Annie and Evie, while the rest would come just in time for the picnic lunch after the cleaning was all done.

"Well, here we go," Addy told Annie after they parked the car and started to walk toward the schoolhouse.

"It won't be bad, Addy," Linc assured her. "There ain't hardly anyone here now that was around when we got kicked out."

"But the feeling may still be here," she answered. Opening the outside door, she went in ahead of the rest.

"Good!" Jessie Anderson called, "More help. Glad to see all of you. Addy, Evie, although I suppose I have to say Miss Parker now. And where are the two little ones?" she asked Annie as she came to meet them.

"I left them at home," Annie answered.

Giving a quick glance over the room, Addy saw many new faces. Those would be the renters of the ranches the government now owned. Lillian Barlow came forward and helped Jessie take the women and Linc around the room to meet everyone. Addy was very pleased and relieved to see the welcome smiles they were receiving.

After filling their pails with warm water and adding a block of homemade soap, Addy and Annie were soon scrubbing. Evie spent her time going through the books that were piled on the back shelves. Linc went outside to help the other men do the outside work. Dan Anderson had brought his team of horses and a hay mower and had mowed off the yard full of dried up tumbling tumbleweeds and prairie grass. When this was done all the men took pitchforks and poked and prodded under and around all the buildings to see if they could find any rattlesnakes that had denned up during the hot summer months.

Some of the men had brought oil cans and hand tools so the merry-go-round and swings could be fixed. About the time this was all done, the women had the work inside done and were ready to put the food out for the picnic dinner.

Addy had told Ted to be at the schoolhouse at noon and she was glad to see his car drive in about five minutes before. Linc helped Ted and Stubby carry in the potato salad Annie had fixed, the yellow cake Evie had baked and the large cinnamon and sugar coffeecake Addy had baked that morning. When the food was passed around, Addy could not help but notice that some of the food told of hardships at home. The bread and jelly sandwiches, large pancakes rolled up with lard and sugar sprinkled inside for filling and corn meal mush slices fried crispy told Addy the renters on the government land had hard pickings. This was verified when one woman, the mother of four school age children with another baby on the way, told of having some of her home canning going to help pay the rent.

"The cattle we sold just didn't sell for enough to make the payment and so part of my canning made up the balance," she said.

"How much rent does the government charge?" someone asked and she answered, "one third of the cattle or whatever you have."

"Jessie," Addy asked quietly, "I was afraid Henry Martin's family would be here today, but I don't see them at all."

"They don't show up to anything. Since that boy of theirs got into all that trouble you don't see hide nor hair of them at anything. Someone said he goes to Casson early in the morning while there ain't nobody around so he don't have to run into anyone he knows."

"I just wondered," Addy said. "It's been fine here today. I was afraid the Martin Family would give us grief. Everyone here has been nice to us."

"This is different from what it used to be, Addy. Got no problems fitting in here. You can see different faces in this community now. I wonder how long Henry will stay around here. Dan and I wonder about that. Oh, they are talking about water for the school. The well here has dried up."

After a lot of discussion, it was finally decided the water would be carried in ten gallon cans from Barlow's. At least, this was how the year would start. There was the possibility that with winter weather something else would have to be worked out.

Addy's biggest worry was how Ken and Pete would be received by the rest of the children. Her fears were laid to rest when she saw how warmly they were welcomed.

"It's going to be great going back to school there," Addy was told by Ken on the way home.

"I think it's going to be great having lots of kids to play with," Pete echoed.

"And how was your day, Evie?" Linc asked. "You ready to take on teaching a large school again?"

"It will be nice," was the reply. "Very nice. Not that I didn't like teaching just two boys, kind of like tutoring. But it is nice to see your family welcomed into the community again and see the boys associating with other children. That is so good for them. Yes, it will be nice."

A week later Stubby and Evie had new problems. The well at their place had dried up and now they had no water for their house and for the cattle Stubby had.

"You'll just have to carry water from here in ten gallon cans, Stubby," Linc said. "But for the stock, I wonder if it wouldn't be better if they were all moved down here until the well has water again."

"Hell. Think I'll just sell the cows. So much more work to haul water. It was so nice to have our own well. I suppose I should have looked for it to happen, what with the dry, hot summer we've had and the ones before this being dry too."

"And Stubby, you ask Evie if she don't want to wash clothes down here. It would be easier. See what she wants to do. Or maybe she would rather wash at home and just carry the water for it. You don't really realize how much water you use until it has to be carried," Addy told him.

"We'll let it go for this year, but next spring I think we should get hold of a witcher and git another well up there," Ted told Stubby.

"A what?" Pete asked.

"A witcher," Ted answered, a big smile creasing his face.

"What's a witcher?" Pete asked looking at Stubby.

"It's a man with water witching knacks that uses a tree

limb to find water below the ground. They hold the limb or stick in front of them just a certain way and when there is water under the ground the stick will bend down toward the ground. Then you dig a well there."

"I never heard of that before. I thought it maybe was a Halloween witch."

"No. These men have a knowledge that is amazing, but it does work. I think by next spring you'll be sick of carrying water," Ted said.

Evie decided to bring her dirty clothes down to Addy's and wash them. It was a nuisance, but still easier than lugging additional water. Stubby sold his stock at the sale barn, but finally decided to keep the chickens.

Addy wanted to visit Martin's grave before winter arrived. Not anxious to go into Casson alone, she had given a lot of thought as to how this was going to be done. Finally she asked Ted to go with her.

"I need salt for the cattle. Maybe I could get it at Casson Feed Mill instead of waiting until the next trip to Linksfort. With finding we are welcome back into the school district maybe I will see how a visit to the feed mill in town here goes. We'll go tomorrow. I wouldn't mind going to the cemetery with you, but maybe you can go alone while I stay at the mill and get the salt. Visit a little and see what happens," Ted answered.

Both felt some anxiety as they drove into Casson. Ted stopped at the feed mill and Addy got into the driver's seat and drove down the streets until she got to the cemetery. Walking slowly across the dry grass, she stopped at the headstone marked Rafferty. Her meditation was shortened when she heard a car stop behind hers. Her heart sunk when she realized it was Pearson, the undertaker.

"Mrs. Rafferty, I am surprised to see you here," he said as he joined her at Martin's grave.

"Why?"

"Just because your husband is laying here, doesn't mean you are welcome here in this town. I only allowed him to be buried here because it was the decent thing to do."

"That was kind of you, I would say," Addy answered.

"Don't get smart with me. He is laying here, but you aren't welcome to come here and I would have thought you would have been smart enough to remember all this."

"You don't own this cemetery, Mr. Pearson," Addy answered.

"Don't tell me what I own and what I don't," he answered shaking his fist at her. Addy flinched as he shouted. "Get out of this town and don't come back again. As long as you are here, you can see the grave, but as I said, don't come back again." Stalking off, he was soon to his car. Looking back he glared at her before getting in and driving off.

Watching his car drive down the block and turn, she noticed another car driving up behind hers. Seeing it was Tom Raymer she went across the cemetery to join him at the cars.

"Hello Tom," she said. "About time for another meeting of the corporation?"

"Hello Addy. Meeting will be shortly after the first of the month. Visiting Martin's grave?"

"I was. I had a visitor."

"I saw. I was coming down the street and when I saw Pearson's car I parked by the side of the street and waited until he was gone. I wondered what he wanted or is he just being nice for a change?"

"Not nice. I can finish visiting the grave now that I am here, but I am never to come back again."

"That pompous fool. I got an idea, Addy. I'd like to think about it further, then meet you somewhere and talk about it. No one else is to know about it. Not any of your kids at all, but it is time to teach him a lesson. Where can I meet you in private?"

"I drive up to Jessie Anderson's often to visit. I drive up through the pasture, not the road, as long as everything is so dry, going up through what used to be Clinton's yard and onto the paved road, up that way. We could meet in Clinton's yard, or what we now call South Ranch."

"Sounds good. Say, day after tomorrow about 1:30 in the afternoon."

"Fine."

Addy wasn't to the feed mill when the constable stopped her, examined her driving license carefully, looked the car over just as carefully and finally let her drive on.

Telling Ted about this, she surmised correctly that Pearson had called the constable's office and told him to harass her. Addy could hardly wait for the day after next to see what Tom Raymer had in mind.

"I've got an idea," Raymer told Addy when they met. "Pearson's got a wife who is foolish. Pearson is self opinionated and thinks highly of himself. But I made a mistake when I called him a fool because he is not. But his wife is. She is bored, not too much for her to do, but go to Casson's high society meetings. Not good looking, but a vain woman. Now, I've got a friend, well not really such a friend, but I go to meetings with him and we eat out occasionally cause I don't like to eat alone all the time. As you know my wife is dead for many years, and after a while, you sometimes eat out with those you don't really like too well, but it is company. Anyway, before I get too carried away with all the details, I have a plan to get those two together, Pearson's wife and my friend, Virgil Jakels. It may take a while because I can't be very pushy. They both will be at a wedding that I am invited to. There is a gathering afterwards at the bride's parents' home and I know both will be there too. Virgil has an eye for wealthy women."

"They must have known each other before now?" Addy asked.

"Yes, but Virgil had a friend, a woman friend that has recently gotten married to someone else and he feels lost. A little nudge in the right direction and it may jell. Pearson won't bother with his wife at all. He just leaves her by herself and I'll tell Virgil that she has money, which she has. Pearson only had the shirt on his back when he married her. She's the one with the money and if she ever left him he'd be broke so fast. She has money coming every month from some trust that was set up for her years ago and still is giving her money."

"How come the Pattons had so much money and Pearson doesn't?" Addy asked.

"Cause the money was on the other side, Pearson's parents didn't have any money."

"Let me know how this is going," Addy told him adding, "Somehow when the next corporation meeting comes, let me know or when you want to meet. I will be all ears. Anything to take him down a peg or two."

"How about burying him in disgrace?"

"Couldn't happen to a better man," Addy agreed laughing.

Several more times that fall, Addy and Tom met in the South Ranch yard. Each time he was able to give Addy a progress report. Yes, Virgil was attracted to Mrs. Pearson and talked to her at the wedding after Tom gave him a gentle nudge. Carefully asking, when the two men went out to eat, Tom was able to find out Mrs. Pearson and Virgil were meeting, very carefully, but were continuing to meet. And with the coming of winter and always more funerals with so much pneumonia and flu, the meeting would be easier and more often. Neither felt Pearson suspected anything.

Tom and Addy met the last time toward the end of October when they agreed they would not meet any more until the following spring. Both hoped something good would come out of all of it besides the obvious pleasure Mrs. Pearson and Virgil were getting.

The previous winter, Addy had found it difficult with Martin so bad and then with his death. But this winter seemed endless to her. Even with all the sewing, knitting, crocheting and embroidering she found the days crept by so slowly. Getting ready for the Christmas season helped pass the month of December. The sewing for the holidays, the shopping at Linksfort for the gifts, the buying of the oranges and fruit for the special treats and extra groceries for the baking and candy making...this all helped the time pass and gave her something different to think about.

For the first time since Martin had gotten sick, Addy felt a desire to go back to her church and Christmas Eve mass. But as long as any of the Patton cousins still lived in Casson and were very prominent yet in the church, Addy knew this was impossible. The old feelings of hatred for the Patton family bubbled in her giving her difficult days of discontentment. All kinds of thoughts of how to get rid of the two last members of that wretched family ran through her mind, but she knew they were only daydreams that could never happen. Finally she thrust all of these thoughts deep within herself and tried to install the Christmas spirit she knew was needed if this was to be a good holiday for the family and especially for her two boys.

The two youngsters of Annie and Linc's were joys to have around. Sara's childish face was constantly wreathed in smiles. Generally her talking could be understood, but when she had repeated something several times and no one understood, she gave up in anger and retreated to sit with her back to everyone and pretend they were not there. This habit of hers brought many a smile. Little Seth, now more than a year old walked early and spent most of his time climbing over everything, much to his ma's concern. Addy made sure, on her last shopping trip to Casson, that she picked up a soft rubber dolly for Sara and a small teddy bear for Seth. I guess it is true, she thought, as she watched the two little ones. Christmas is for children. How Martin would have enjoyed them, when his mind had been right and if he had lived that long. Such a waste, such a waste.

January brought, along with the two major blizzards, the annual job of butchering. More than a week was spent on this job and everyone was glad that it was over and done with.

"The same thing every year, over and over," Annie said as they finished washing up the washtubs and big pots and pans. "You would think I would remember how to do all of this by now, but I forget from year to year."

"Maybe I'll write it all down for you, just in case."

"Why?" Annie asked. "You planning to not be here next year?"

"I hope so, but you never know. So I guess I'll just get it all written down and then you'll know exactly what to do, when to do it and how to do it."

"Ma, you scare me when you talk like that," Annie told her.

"Look, I mean to be here for some time, but now I know that things can happen so it's just smart to take care of it while I can. Anyway, maybe the day will come and I may not remember either what comes next." Wiping off the stove, Addy added, "Anyway, I want to be here for a while yet just to watch those little ones of yours grow. They are a joy to me."

"I'm glad you think so. Linc and I do too. Ma, we know Ted sees a lot of Nellie. You think he'll marry her?"

"I hope so. She fits in here so good. And there would be a place for them to live too."

"River Ranch's buildings," Annie said. "Yes, that would be a nice place for them."

"You wish you had someplace else? Away from the big house here and all the people? Somewhere else to live?" Addy asked as they finished the final dishes.

"No. I'm happy here. It would seem funny to live where there was no one around most of the time. I'm used to seeing people around and it would be lonely somewhere else."

"I'm glad, cause there are more people here."

"It's not like you're all living with us. I wouldn't like to have to share a house with all of you. That would be a different story."

"I wouldn't like that either," Addy agreed.

"And as far as Ted and Nellie are concerned, I guess we'll have to wait and see what happens there."

"Maybe he'll give her an engagement ring for Valentines Day," Addy said, her eyes sparkling. "That would be nice."

"Yes, that would be something nice," Annie agreed. "Or maybe no ring cause they cost a lot of money. I'm glad I got mine and got married before this depression got so bad."

Indeed, Valentines Day did bring a small engagement ring on Nellie's finger. And a wedding date already picked out.

"Oh Ted, I'm so glad," Addy said as she gave him a hug, and then hugging Nellie she added, "I'm so glad you're going to be in the family."

"So am I," Nellie said.

"And we've picked out a day already for the wedding," Ted told them.

"We want to get married the eighteenth of June," Nellie said.

"And we want to live at River Ranch. I hope that is all right with everybody," Ted added.

"It is just fine. Annie and I talked about it while we were finishing dishes from the butchering and we thought that would be where you would live when you did get married. You've got to tell the renters when they have to move," Addy reminded him.

"I'm going to do that next time I get up there. I don't think it will be a problem with them cause they figured to stay there only a little while when they moved in. The house will need cleaning up. Nellie figured that she will have time to do that after school gets out this spring."

"Where you going to get married?" Annie asked.

"I don't know yet, probably by a judge in Linksfort. I never ever thought that is how I'd get married, but we can't go to church anywhere now, not welcome anywhere and Nellie ain't got a church she goes to so I guess we'll just have it done by a judge."

"If you ever get it straightened out in your church, Ted, then I think I would like to go with you. I never was taught much religion. Ma and Pa never did go much, even when they had a church of their own. So maybe in time, we'll have a church to go to. I think I'd like that," Nellie said holding out her hand for Ted to squeeze.

"There will be no going to church in Casson as long as any Patton relatives live in that town," Addy said adding, "They seem like pretty permanent fixtures, part of the town forever and ever and ever."

Addy put thoughts of the coming wedding on hold as she had to get ready for the March corporation meeting that would be held at her house. She wondered if Tom would have any progress to report on Mrs. Pearson and Virgil. She hadn't seen him since October when they last met at South Ranch.

"Aw, here's Tom now," Dave Lay said as the group watched the kitchen door open. "You're always earlier than the rest of us. We began to wonder if you were coming when it got so late."

"Got a flat tire on the car. Good thing it is cold outside today. Sure wouldn't drive if the roads were like they were last week. It was so muddy that we'd have been stuck for sure."

"Well, let's get started with this," Dave said, giving everyone their copies of the financial statements.

"First things, first. I have some news that just can't keep," Tom said looking at Addy and winking. "Our good undertaker's wife, Mrs. Pearson, has run off with Virgil Jakels!"

"Run off, like left?" Linc asked, astonishment all over his face.

"Just like that. They ran off Sunday morning. Sunday of all days, when those good people always went to church. Seems she felt funny that morning, faint I was told. Thought she should stay home from church. When he got back she was gone. Left a note for him saying she had left with Virgil."

"Glory be," Addy said, her mouth broke into a smile. "Now what happens?"

"He took out after her. Guess he felt she would go back to her people in Oregon and he called out there and they said that is where she was going. She had a friend in town, lady friend in Casson, that told my sister this. She had written her people saying she was coming back and they made the mistake of telling Pearson this and so he went out there too. I sure wish I could see that meeting when they all get together."

"He never paid any attention to her before. Why start now?" Leo Arnold asked.

"Cause she has the money, not him but her. When they got married everyone said he married her cause she has money. Has a check coming in monthly from some trust. He hasn't got the money, she has."

"It will be interesting to see what happens next. Do you think she'll come back with Pearson?" Addy asked Tom.

"No, I don't. Virgil has paid a lot of attention to her. Pearson treated her like she was nothing. And from what I have heard, Virgil treated her like a queen. I don't think she'll want to come back here and be treated like dirt again."

"Interesting, most interesting!" Addy commented smiling broadly.

By the first of May, Casson had another funeral director. Pearson came back only as long as it took to sell his business. The story he told was of going into partnership with his cousin who was in the furniture making business. Nothing was mentioned about his wife's whereabouts, but most surmised that without her money, he could not keep the expensive home they had and he would not be seen in Casson living in anything smaller or cheaper.

"Pride has it's failing," Addy commented when told this. "And I will not cry a tear. Now maybe I can stand by Martin's grave without being chased out."

"Still got one more of Patton's cousins in town yet, Addy," Ted told her. "The Casson postmaster and he is a Patton through and through."

"Yes, I know," she answered.

The first warm days of May, Addy was ready to tackle the painting of the rest of the house that had not been done last spring. Several new rugs had been braided during the winter months. Those would be laid on the floors after the final coatings of varnish. She knew she had finally turned the corner and life seemed worth living again.

"Ken and I know what you need, Ma, to get out of the humdrum," Pete told her one Sunday morning, the end of May. "Just look at that sun and just think how nice it would be along the river fishing for all those good eating fish."

"You hungry for fish?" she asked.

"Yes. And we thought maybe you'd like to learn how to fish for them. Would you, Ma?" Pete asked.

"Learn to fish? Me? I never fished in my life," she answered raising both eyebrows.

"You're old enough to learn how now," Pete told her.

Addy burst into laughter, and much to his chagrin gave him a huge hug. "I wouldn't know the first thing about it."

"You could learn, Ma," Ken coaxed.

"If you really want me to go, then I will go along." Seeing the look that passed between the two boys, she added, "And I will try to catch a fish."

The first thing Addy had to learn was how to bait the hook. Taking the squirming worm in her fingers, she finally managed to get the job done.

"If you could see your face," Ken told her as both boys laughed.

"If it is all screwed up in dislike, then you know how I felt about doing that to that poor worm."

"Only way to catch a fish is to give it some bait," Pete answered throwing his line into the water.

"Now that's how I'm supposed to do it?" Addy asked.

"Yeah, only be careful so you don't catch your hook in those branches above you," Ken answered. "See, you throw it out like this."

Numerous tries finally netted Addy a large bullhead, followed by a second one, soon followed by a medium sized carp. All in all, she caught seven fish. She was elated and after telling the rest of the family about her experience, she did find it was a satisfying and delightful day.

"I do believe I have found something more to do with my time that I really enjoy," she told them all in wonderment. "I can't believe I really enjoyed it so much. Thank you boys for asking me along."

"I believe you would call it begging, Ma," Pete told her. "And now of course we got to clean them. You always told us that whatever we caught we had to clean."

"Everything comes back to haunt you, don't it?" she said, trying to give him a quick squeeze. "Go in and get the knives and I'll do my share."

"I can't hardly wait for you to pickle that carp," Ted told her.

"It will be good, won't it?" Addy answered.

"Last year you learned to drive a car and this year you learned to fish. What else you going to learn how to do?" Linc asked.

"I do know I'm going to ride Baldy more this year. I thought about that this winter and I decided to ride a lot more, even if I have to go alone."

"Good idea," Linc agreed.

"I'd ride with you, Ma, but I think my babies are too small yet," Annie told her.

"I think so too," Linc agreed, but added words of caution. "Addy be sure when you are fishing or riding that you watch out for wild animals that have rabies. We haven't seen any yet this year, but that don't mean there won't be. Dan and David both said their dogs have already tangled with porcupines. Dan said he had to pull out quite a few from his dog's mouth. David said his had only a few, but he supposed the dog hadn't learned anything yet and wouldn't until he had his mouth and nose plumb full. His dog is a young pup and full of vim and vigor, so it's bound to happen living that close to the river."

"Yeah!" Addy agreed. "It took Shep a while before he finally learned to leave porcupines alone. Martin spent the better part of one day, a few years ago, just getting his nose and mouth cleaned out. He cut off the quills too to make them easier to pull and still the dog suffered so. Was sick for a few days. Never went near them after that."

"Anyway, just watch animals that don't act right," Linc cautioned again.

"I will," Addy assured him.

Watching Addy walk off to help Pete clean the fish, Linc told Annie, "You know something? Your ma is quite a lady."

CHAPTER IX

Addy looked forward to Ted's wedding with mixed emotions. She was happy for Ted and glad he had picked out such a good woman like Nellie. Her family and Addy's family were not only close neighbors, but very good friends. The two families discussed at length the wedding invitation list. Barlow's had some close relatives living near or in Linksfort. Addy's family had none close so that was simple. There was further discussion of which neighbors and friends to put on the list. Addy and her family had discussed at length what to do about the corporation members, but when Addy made mention of knowing these people and wondering what to do about inviting them, the Barlows said they knew them well enough too, so they should be added. Barlow bought machinery from Raymer, they banked with Lay's bank and knew him quite well, and Barlow had bought wheat from Leo Arnold. Since then the two families had gotten together for several Sunday visits.

The wedding plans were simple. Money being the main factor, the Barlows planned for a plain wedding dinner following the eleven o'clock wedding service at their home.

Everyone was invited to eat and then spend the afternoon.

Addy had already shopped at Linksfort for material for her dress, finally deciding on a lovely blue flowered material. After a lot of hesitation she took two patterns and used part of each.

"That should make up real pretty, Ma," Annie told her after she showed it to both Annie and Nellie.

"I like the collar you're putting on the dress. It adds so much and will make it look elegant," Nellie added.

"Elegant, now that is not a word I would have used for any of my clothes," Addy laughed.

"You will look very nice. You and my ma will be the best looking people there right after Annie and me," Nellie teased.

"What are you wearing, Annie?" Nellie asked.

"I took my wedding dress and fixed it up a little. Added here and took off there and I think it will be all right. It is a pale green so it won't look like a wedding dress."

"It looks real nice," Addy told her. "I want to get a new hat. My hats are old and I just want a new one. If I can't find anything that I like, then I'll get plain white material and cover one of my old ones. I like that cloche one, that old brown one so well. It fits nicely and if I cover it in white, it will go fine."

"You should look first," Nellie told her.

"I will. Evie is going to stay with the two little ones one day next week and Annie and I are going to Linksfort and shop. Linc is going too, at least I hope so. He said I could drive, but I don't know if I want to go that far, just the two of us without a man along. He seemed to think we'd be alright."

"You have driven in town?" Nellie slowly asked.

"Oh yes. Linc and Ted have both made me drive in Linksfort lots of times when I went with them. I don't mind it at all now," Addy answered.

"We offered Evie a place to stay this fall when school starts," Nellie told them. "It was so hard for her to get to school so much of the time last winter and with us living so close to the school, we just thought it would be nice if she wanted to stay at our house during the cold months."

"What did she say?" Addy asked. "She ain't said anything to me about it."

"We just talked to her today. She said that was really nice and she would take us up on it only during the cold weather and bad roads though. She felt newly wedded people needed privacy to get to know each other," Nellie answered.

"She's a sweet lady," Annie smiled. "Can be sharp if needed, but underneath a sweet lady."

"And very correct," Addy added. "I said one day, while we were hoeing in the garden, how nice it would be if women could wear pants or overalls like men do when we were working outside and she told me in a hurry that women dressed like women and that was that. She had enough to do without worrying about something like that."

"You wear pants while you ride and when you go fishing with Ken and Pete," Annie told her.

"Then I guess that it is alright, but not working in the garden or if you had to work in the barn or even making hay like some of the women do, working on top of loads of hay stacking."

"Well, she does have some old fashioned straight laced ideas, but she is a good woman," Annie said.

"I know she will do as much as she can to stay out of our way when she does have to stay with us this coming winter," Nellie told them.

"Say, there is something we have to do yet, and that is to find someone to stay here while we're gone on your wedding day," Annie said. "Linc and Ted both thought they would ask Dave Lay if he knew of anyone that could come here for the day."

"Maybe Stubby will have some relative or friend. He seems to know most everybody around Linksfort," Nellie said.

"He did mention someone. The men will come up with somebody I'm sure. They were talking yesterday about several ranchers having cattle stolen, ranches way north of here. Just drove trucks onto the back of the ranches and loaded up the cattle. Made some sort of a make-shift corral," Addy said.

"Many at a time?" Nellie asked. "Pa never mentioned anything about this."

"He probably ain't heard about it. Ted just mentioned it this morning," Addy answered.

"Linc said some of the ranchers are finding where cattle have been butchered right out in the pasture. Usually one or two at a time. Thought probably the quarters were sold to a butcher shop somewhere. Maybe the people, the thieves, even kept part of the meat for themselves," Annie told them.

"But this is hot weather and the meat won't keep unless you have ice for it," Addy said.

"Linc said the guy who told him figured they probably sold it right away to a butcher shop. Butchered it at night and hauled it to a butcher shop that knew they were coming with the stolen meat."

"Anything for a few bucks," Addy answered. "Just anything at all."

The eighteenth of June was warm, sunny and just the right kind of a day for a wedding. The two men Dave Lay had suggested for staying at the home ranch drove in just as Addy had finished dressing. Ken and Pete were already in their new clothes.

"You both look so nice," Addy told them. "New shirts and trousers, even new socks and new shoes."

"I never had a pair of shoes like this, Ma. And it's been a long time since I had a new white shirt and good trouser pants," Ken answered.

"I know, ever since we stopped going to church," she replied.

"We'll leave for Barlow's as soon as Linc shows the men around outside. I've got to tell them what to eat while we're gone," Addy said.

"What time we gonna be back?" Pete asked.

"By chore time. Lillian plans to serve a lunch to everyone before they leave this afternoon. We'll be back by five o'clock. Plenty of time to do chores. I'll drive our car so it won't be so crowded."

Although Addy had looked forward to the day with mixed emotions, she found she thoroughly enjoyed herself. The wedding service was very simple. Linc served as best man while Nellie's cousin was maid of honor.

Nellie's wedding dress was made of white silk. Although the design was simple, the lace collar and matching lace sleeves trimmed with buttons looked beautifully eloquent. White shoes and a large white bow topping her red hair completed the outfit.

Bartons had planned the dinner seating very well. The garage served as a dining room with planks placed over the tops of sawhorses for tables. Homemade benches were used instead of chairs. The wedding party and the parents were privileged to eat in the house while everyone else sat in the garage.

After the main meal was over the rest of the afternoon was filled with card playing, visiting and playing for the smaller children. Ken and Pete had brought along their checker and Chinese checker games to help fill the time. They both knew playing ball was not in order for the day. Their ma would not be pleased to see them roughing it in their new white shirts and dark pants she had just finished sewing.

Just before leaving, Tom Raymer had asked Addy to meet him the following day at South Ranch yard. Maybe, just maybe, they could make plans for the removal of the last of the Patton cousins. Addy could hardly wait for the next day.

"I don't know if it will work," he told her the following afternoon. "It's a long shot, but worth a try. I just hate to go to the post office any more. I can hardly stand to look at Arthur Loging. He's so much like Ray Patton, looks like him and acts like him and I have had my fill of it."

"What do you have in mind?" Addy asked.

"One of the big wheels, farther up in the postal system, has a wife that has tuberculosis, TB. She has been moved to a sanitarium because they can't stay home with that." Addy nodded her head in agreement. "His car broke down a couple of months ago and he don't have the money to get another one, what with paying for her care where she is. My brother told me about this when we had a family reunion picnic about two weeks ago Sunday. I asked my brother if there would be the possibility of buying the man a car...in return...for his moving Loging out of here."

"Is there another job somewhere to move Loging to?" Addy asked, listening intently.

"Yes, there is," Tom answered. "It's a town way east of here."

"But no guarantee comes with the offer of the car that Loging would leave?" Addy asked.

"None, unless that is part of the bargain. And here again, we have to find the money for buying the car. I would be willing to put up half of the money if you could find the other half. I don't have enough money to pay for all of it. I figure $50.00 will get him a good car. Good 1929 Model A Ford Roadsters are selling for around that price."

"How do we know he won't come back and ask us for more money, blackmail us?"

"He won't know where the car is coming from. And my brother would work that out. And I trust my brother with my life. He lived here and went to school with Arthur and knew him very well. He was a smart aleck then just like he is now. And something else in our favor, he has daughters ready to go to college and the town where he would go has a college there. That might be an added point with his wife. Be in our favor."

"If $50.00 will move him out of here for good, I can find half the money."

"Without anyone knowing about it?" Tom asked.

"Yes. I have some money of my own. Been using a little here and there when I needed something extra like paint for the downstairs of the house. No one else knows what there is left. I just didn't want to take out of ranch funds. Yes, I can get the money."

"All right. Let me work on this further. We have a corporation meeting in about a week. I'll try to get there early and tell you what happened."

"Annie is usually there before anyone else to get the children settled for their naps."

"Then I'll meet you here in two weeks. Two weeks from today." With that he got into his car and left. After Addy untied Baldy's reins from the fence, she stood a few minutes thinking until the horse nudged her with his nose.

"Ready to go home, old boy?" she asked gently stroking his face. "You're one fine horse."

Even with all the work Addy found to do, along with several afternoons of fishing, rides on Baldy, driving the car for visits to Nellie's, Lillian's and Jessie's, the two weeks until the next meeting with Tom dragged on leaded wheels. Addy knew she shouldn't get her hopes high for the removal of the last of the Patton family, but if he were gone then she could go back to her church. They could shop in Casson again and they would be free to go and come as they pleased. It would be like a dream after the long nightmare.

At last the day of the meeting came. Although it looked like rain, Addy rode Baldy to South Ranch. She had to wait just a few minutes before Tom drove in.

"It looks good, Addy. Looks good. I am hopeful, very hopeful. I made a special trip down to see my brother right after we met last time and he did some further inquires and checking. The man, whose wife has the TB, would be very glad for a car, no strings attached. He would not know where it came from, but he would not get the car unless Loging moved. That was one of the stipulations, one of the conditions."

"I would like that if he didn't know. I don't want him ever coming back after more money. I don't care how good a person he might be, when you get short of money, then you go looking where you have to," Addy said.

"Granted, that is true. The car would be delivered to his home. He lives on the outskirts of town. According to my brother he has a barn and other buildings. They have horses and a few cows. No one would even notice, especially if the car was dropped off at night. So he would have no idea who brought it."

"I never asked where this opening came from that Loging would be moved up to?" Addy asked.

"A fellow died quite suddenly. It hasn't been filled yet. I suppose someone from the post office there figures to get the job, but I can't let my conscience bother me on that subject. If Loging takes this job, he would have a boss over him. That kind of appeals to me."

"Right," Addy agreed.

"So now we wait and see if Loging picks up the bait," Tom told her.

"Any idea how long?"

"No. I know the position has to be filled within a certain time frame, but I don't know how long and my brother didn't either."

"So we wait."

"Let us meet again in two weeks. You know, when this is finally settled and I hope the way we want, I am going to miss these meetings. I have enjoyed them."

"So have I. You always know the news from Casson. I fill you in on what goes on here and what I know of Linksfort. And it is nice having someone to visit with."

"Oh say, about news, we have a new priest. And he's been checking all the books from way back, checking to see who moved and just checking up on the parishioners. He asked at a council meeting about you people and Loging told him why you didn't go to church here anymore. In no uncertain terms, from what I hear. And Father Masonick asked him who gave them the authority for their family to say who can and can't go to church there? And Loging got up and left fuming and blustering all the way out the door."

"Maybe that will help him decide to leave Casson," Addy

said, "I can't believe someone finally stood up to that family."

"I guess Father Masonick really was sarcastic. I'd have liked to have heard it, but I'm not part of the Council anymore so I missed it."

"It looks like I had better go back. Rain seems very close. Two weeks, then we meet again." Tom nodded yes. "I hope something good comes out of this. And I will bring money next time, just in case."

"No don't. If I need it, I can meet you the next day or as soon as it is needed."

Addy was nervous, anxious and sharp tongued, so unlike her, during the following week. Finally Ken remarked about it one noon after getting raked over the coals over a very minor incident.

"I didn't think I did anything wrong this noon when I didn't pick the eggs. They were picked at the middle of the morning and some days they are picked before dinner and some days afterwards. Ted wanted me to help him finish loading the wagon with wood and we didn't get done until it was too late to pick the eggs before dinner." Looking defiantly at his ma, he added, "I'll go do it now. I don't want any dinner. I'll live without eating. I'd rather not have any than to get hollered at all through the meal."

"Sit down there young man!" Addy shouted, then put her head in her hands and giving a big sigh, she apologized. "I'm sorry, Ken. Really I am. I don't know what is the matter with me. Yes, I do know, but it ain't something you can do anything about. Eat your dinner and pick the eggs afterwards and I'll try to be a better ma from now on. Truly, I am sorry."

After dinner, Addy saddled Baldy and rode north onto the gumbo. She rode the dividing line between Big Mile Ranch and High Ranch where Stubby and Linc were busy digging a dam with the Allis Chalmers tractor. She spent time just watching them work, then rode farther west until she came to the fence between High Ranch and the next ranch. Turning south she followed the line fence for some miles until realizing she would be late for supper, she turned Baldy toward home. By the time she reached the main buildings, she had her nerves under control.

"Ma, you took a long ride," Annie told her after she had let Baldy loose in the pasture and was walking across the yard toward the house.

"I went up to see the new dam and then rode for a while after that," she answered.

"Everything all right now?" Annie asked.

"Yes. Ken must have told you I was crabby, huh?"

"He did mention it," Annie answered smiling. "And I have noticed you sure are jumpy."

"It's better now. Hopefully whatever it is will get out of my system pretty soon," she answered continuing to the house.

Addy had a visitor the following morning. He wore a black suit and had a white collar.

"Oh my," she murmured to herself, hurrying to the door. "I'll bet it is the new priest at St. Johns."

And it was. He strode up the path, knocked on the door and waited for Addy to open it.

"Mrs. Rafferty?" he asked.

"Yes, and I would believe you are Father Masonick," Addy answered.

"You know who I am?"

"I guessed. Come on in," she said stepping aside so he could enter the room. "You just surprised me. I wasn't looking for you to come and see us."

"And why not?" he asked.

"Just because, I guess. I just didn't look for you to come." She shrugged as she offered him a chair. "I'll get you a cup of coffee. Just made a fresh pot for breakfast. If you drink coffee, that is?"

"I'd be glad for a cup. Yes, that is one of my sins. I do enjoy my coffee. You have a nice ranch here. Someone told me you also own land up on the gumbo and even bought some of the ranches when they came up on sheriff's sale."

"Yes, we did. You see, some time ago I inherited some

money and that is what was used."

"I didn't mean to imply that you had a great amount of wealth. No one seems to have that now in this great depression. I was just commenting, I guess."

"And I just answered as to where the money came from to buy the land with. My late husband always felt land was a good place to put money. And so when the opportunity came to buy some, we did. I felt good about it then and I still do."

"My people come from the land. My parents are farmers back in Minnesota. I came out here to go to the seminary and stayed here when I was ordained, but I know how my pa feels about his farm. And I imagine you feel the same about your ranches. He milks cows, sells milk to a creamery."

"We only keep a few milk cows so we have milk for the houses. And now with Ted married, he keeps two milk cows at his house. I am glad you understand and are from a farm. Then you know and understand us better."

"Now, I have been looking back through all the records of St. Johns and I find a few years ago that you quit coming to church and I wondered why. I hope to resolve that problem and get you and your family back in the fold, the parish."

"Father, I left because I was not comfortable anymore going to church. I was not welcome nor were any of my family. Do you know any of the history or background of why we were shoved out of Casson?"

"Yes. I have talked to several about it. I talked to Tom Raymer. I talked to several others of the Council, who have been in the town for some time. I also talked to Arthur Loging, or rather he talked to me."

"Yes, I would imagine he would. So what and who did you believe?"

"I believed all of them because basically they all told the same story. Loging, his cousin, Pearson, can't remember what his first name was, and brothers, Ray and Joe Patton forced your family out of Casson. I haven't yet figured out how they did this. I haven't gotten the full story of how they did this...how they got so powerful that they could force people to follow them."

"Joe was the banker. He had a lot of money loaned to various businesses in Casson. Ray was a rancher, but also had a lot of money loaned to other ranchers in this area. Joe and Ray just told the ones that owed them money that if they were friendly to us, even talked to us, that they would pull in their loans, foreclose on them."

"Oh! Yes, I guess that would work."

"And they also had a hold over Father Johnson, the priest that was here before you. The last time I went to church, Father Johnson turned his back on me when I came out the church door as he was greeting everyone who was leaving church. That was not a chance turning away. That was on purpose. I know from the financial statements that came every year with the bulletin that Joe and Ray Patton's and their cousins, but especially Joe and Ray were big givers to the church. I thought when Father Johnson did that to me that I was never going back again and I didn't," Addy told him.

"And when the bank closed it's doors, Ray shot Joe and then killed himself. How come Ray shot Joe and then himself? If the bank went down, Ray would still have had the ranches in this area to keep him financially stable. I don't understand what happened there." Father questioned.

"Shortly before the bank closed it's doors, Ray sold his ranch, moved to town and decided to run for state senator. Actually he decided that before he moved. He took the mortgages he had, turned them over to the bank for cash. He used some of the money for his political campaign and put the rest in the bank under interest. He got money from the sale of his ranch by us here, but as I understood it, most of it went to buy the fancy house he bought and the rest went for his campaign. He must have decided he needed more money for politics than he had so he sold the mortgages on the other ranches near here to the bank. Joe didn't want him to use the money he had under interest at the bank from before when he sold several large ranches in South Dakota. I would imagine, as hard to come by as money is these days, that there isn't too much extra money floating around in the political area either. Anyway, that is what happened. So the community was rid of two of the Pattons."

"But the two cousins were still in Casson," Father commented.

"Yes. I don't know if you are into scandals, but the undertaker Pearson's wife ran off with a man from Casson, a Virgil Jackel. She was the one who had the money, had money coming in every month from some trust started by someone long ago. Anyway, every month a check came to her and since she ran away with another man, that left Pearson without money. The funeral parlor business don't make much money. I think that is like everything else. Just keeps it's head above water, so to say. Anyway, he came back after he went out to Oregon to try to get her back. He came back long enough to sell the business, and went by his cousin or some relative who makes furniture. That is what he is doing as far as we know."

"And that leaves only Arthur Loging," Father slowly added.

"And that leaves Loging," Addy agreed. "And as long as he is here and going to St. Johns, I will not come back. I have to say, whether you like to hear it or not, I have an immense hatred for the people in Casson, for the old neighbors around here and especially for the Pattons. You can't imagine how hard life was. My husband was sick, sick in the head. And with that to look at, him getting worse and worse and then no one talking to us, or very few that is, my liking for the people here in this area turned to hatred. And that is another reason why I was glad to buy the land. It put a cushion around my home. It made those that hated us farther away."

"Not many of those are left now, are they?" he asked.

"No. My boys are back in the school again." He raised his

eyebrows at this comment. "Oh, Ray Patton and two of his friends, rather two men that he held mortgages on their ranch. They were brothers-in-laws and ranched together. Patton loaned them money. They were the school board and they came and told me to keep my boys home from school. They would not be responsible for them if they got hurt in school from others fighting with them. We hired a school teacher to teach my boys here at home. Her brother came and worked for us too. They live in the house across the road above the highway. You can see it when you go back. The buildings lay right below the hill. They live in that house cause we own that land. Now Evie teaches school in the school we were thrown out of. Evie is the teacher I hired to teach my sons."

"I haven't been told why Pattons had such a fear of you."

"Fear?" Addy asked.

"Oh yes, it is a fear when you act like that," Father answered.

"Well maybe you are right. We learned this after the Patton brothers died. Their grandma had the same thing Martin, my husband had. The family had a great fear of this sickness. After she died, in a few years Ray and Joe's ma got the same thing as her ma had. Their pa, Ray and Joe's pa, bought the ranch where Ray lived. He moved out there to get the woman out of town because she was walking the streets and didn't know where she was. He was ashamed of her, didn't want anyone to know how she was. Some say he left her wander anywhere when they got on the ranch. One day she got into a pen with a bull and was trampled to death. Some said he left her go in there on purpose. But that was only hearsay. Ray and Joe were brought up with a great fear of anyone with that sickness. So they wanted to get us out of here so they wouldn't even have to look at anyone that was sick in the head. Like if it was gone out of sight, then we were all right."

"Out of sight, out of mind," Father said.

"Yes, something like that," Addy agreed. "Life was very miserable during those days. We took all our business to

Linksfort, everything was done at that town, including our post office box. The only place we go in Casson now is the feed mill. Martin is buried in Casson, in the family plot, but when I went to see his grave after he died, Pearson kicked me out of the cemetery."

"Oh my! That does explain a lot."

"I will not come back to St. Johns as long as Arthur Loging is in Casson. And we ain't welcome at the cathedral at Linksfort either."

"I suppose because of boundaries. Did you explain what happened?" he asked.

"I didn't. But when Linc and Annie's Sara was born, Annie wanted her baptized and they refused to do it. So neither of their babies are baptized. And when Ted got married, he was married by a judge. That was this summer. And neither Ken or Pete are getting any religious training other than what I have taught them. Ken should be confirmed now, but that won't be done either. And Martin was buried out of this house, with the funeral director saying a few prayers and my family saying a few the night before by ourselves. So now maybe you see why I am filled with hatred for that family," Addy told him, her eyes flashing.

He rubbed his chin, sat a moment thinking and then asked "And when Loging leaves town that will be the end of the Pattons?"

"That is the last one. He is as strong in his belief in their ways as any one of them. Probably stronger because he is the last and feels he must uphold what they felt so strongly," Addy answered.

"Rumors have it that he is leaving for another job. Been offered a job in another post office eastern part of the state. He feels it is not any better than the one he has, not a step up in his career. Here, he is his own boss and there he will have a boss over him. I guess there is a college in that town and his daughters want dearly to go there to further their education. And their mama wants them to go there and has been leaning heavily on Arthur to move. She feels it would be a step in the right direction, I was told."

"Is he going to go?" Addy asked her heart beating faster with each word.

"I was told he would make the decision by the end of this week."

"I can only hope it is yes. Dearly hope so," Addy said.

"My guess is that he will. That family is losing their grip on the town. By that I mean the Pattons are losing the iron hand they had in running Casson. I for one do not fall in line with Loging's thinking and he knows it. I will not bow down to anything like that. I do my own thinking. He is the last one of that family. And by being offered this job, he can leave with dignity."

"I can hardly wait."

"I'd like to meet the rest of your family, if I may?" Father implored.

"I can introduce you to Annie, my daughter. She married my step-son Linc."

"Yes, I found that in the records."

"Oh, I suppose," Addy agreed. "We'll go down to their house. They live in the house on the edge of this yard, a little ways off from the rest of the buildings. And Ted is here somewhere. Linc, Ken and Pete went up to Big Mile Ranch to check cattle and pasture. They won't be back until later. I have to take them up dinner today."

"By horse back?" he asked.

"No, I drive the car." He looked surprised so Addy added, "I have a drivers license and do a lot of driving. I go to Linksfort occasionally with Annie or Evie. Just the two women. I found that I was the envy of some of the women when I drove my boys to school. Not all of them. Some of the men didn't think it was very proper to have a woman drive, but then that is their problem," Addy added smiling slightly, "And so let's go and see who we can find today for you to meet."

Addy was anxious for the meetings with Tom before this, but now she could hardly wait to hear what news he would bring. She kept telling herself not to get her hopes too high, but each time she went over Father Masonick's conversation she felt new surges of hope.

Knowing she was leaving too early the meeting day, she deliberately took the long way to the South Ranch meeting place. Even so she had minutes to wait until she saw Tom's car coming down the road.

"Good, bad or in between?" she asked as he got out of the car.

"Good! The weather? It's fine today. Bad? Not the weather. In between? No I would say it is sunny, warm and a generally good day," he teased, smiling broadly as he watched the expression on her face.

"That's not what I want to know. I know what the weather is. Father Masonick was to see me and I want to know if you think the same as he does. Or if things have happened as he thought maybe they would." Addy answered.

"And what did he think would happen?" Tom asked.

"He felt that Loging would leave, take that job. Reason one: his wife was pushing it. Reason two: the daughters want to go to college there. Reason three: the Patton influence was dimming, not great or strong and he was the last one and could not keep it going. Reason four: he could take the job and leave Casson in dignity. That was his version."

"And he was one hundred percent right. All of that did happen. They are moving the end of the month."

"Ten days. Ten more days," Addy shouted, waving her arms in happiness. "Ten more days."

"A miracle. Did you bring money today?" he asked.

"Yes. I know you told me not to, but from what the good priest said and what I hoped and hoped, I took a chance and did bring the money."

"Good. I'll take it back and make the trip to my brother's tomorrow with it and then we are finished with all of that. And so that comes to an end. Were you surprised to see Father Masonick?"

"Oh yes," Addy answered and then began to relate to him all that had happened since she had last visited with him.

Two weeks later, Linc came back from the feed mill with the news of the departure of the Arthur Loging family.

"And would you believe it, Addy," he said. "They only rented that house. They didn't even own it. Everyone was wondering if they would leave before they sold the house and then they found out that they only rented it."

"Maybe they didn't have as much money as everyone thought," Addy said. "But it was fixed up really nice from what I heard. Who did own it?"

"Someone from north of here somewhere. They visited here once when the house was for sale and bought it and then asked Loging to live in it until they retired and moved here. And Loging just kept renting it. Whoever owned it kept the house fixed up. Whenever it needed painting, Loging had it painted and papered inside and the owner paid for it. No wonder they could keep it nice. Someone else foot the bill."

"Can't beat it, can you?" Addy answered. "So they actually have left. You're sure of this?"

"They have gone. New renters are moving in next month. They have gone."

"Then I am going to Casson this afternoon and go to the cemetery."

"Want someone to go with you?" Linc asked. "Maybe Annie and the youngsters can go with you."

"No, I want to go alone," Addy answered. "I made a promise to myself and to Martin after Pearson kicked me out of the cemetery that day. I promised myself that after there were no more Pattons in Casson that I would go back to see Martin and his grave. And now the last one is gone. I'm going to keep that promise."

The sun shone warmly on Addy as she stood by Martin's grave. Long minutes passed as she looked around. Stooping down she pulled out the weeds and grass that threatened to cover the bottom of the headstone. Lovingly, her hands caressed the cold stone as she finally felt at peace.

Noticing a car pulling up behind hers on the road, she saw that it was Tom Raymer's. He stood at the edge of the cemetery while she walked toward him.

"Everything all right, Addy?" he asked.

"Everything is fine, Tom," she replied. "Finally! It took so long, but now I feel at peace with myself and my world is healed."

Putting her hand in his, they walked slowly toward the cars.